"You mean you didn't tell your parents?" David asked.

"No. I was going to, but then Carrie said if I squealed on her, she'd run away again—and this time she wouldn't come back."

"And you believed her?"

"Sure I believed her."

He looked at me like I was crazy—like I was the one with the problem, not Carrie.

"She did it before," I yelled. "Remember? She disappeared for five whole months and we didn't know if she was dead or alive! It was horrible, Murdock! Do you hear me? Horrible! And I never want to go through that again!"

My eyes filled with tears. I had to get away from him . . . away from the memories . . . away from the gut-wrenching fear that it could all happen again.

The sequel to

MISSING:
Carrie Phillips, Age 15

Don't Tell Mom

written by

Janet Dagon

digital cover illustration by

Michael Petty

For Tracey—
who made it all possible

PAGES
Publishing Group

Fifth printing by Willowisp Press 1997.

Published by PAGES Publishing Group
801 94th Avenue North, St. Petersburg, Florida 33702

Cover illustration © 1997 by PAGES Publishing Group

Printed in the United States of America

6 8 10 9 7 5

ISBN 0-87406-874-6

Chapter

one

"HOW about this one?" my friend, Lisa, asked, pulling another dress off the rack. It was an orange strapless job with a big, black bow at the waist. I crinkled my face and stuck out my tongue.

"Oh, come on, Amy, what's wrong with it?" she asked.

"Nothing, Lis. I always wanted to look like the Great Pumpkin."

"Well, that's it," she said, shoving the dress back in place. "We've looked at every dress on every rack in every store in the mall. If you haven't found anything you like by now . . ."

She looked at me, shaking her head in a slow kind of way. I hated when she did that. She looked like my mother.

"You're making it sound like it's now or never," I said, leaning against the mirror behind me. "The dance is still two weeks away.

I've got plenty of time to come up with something."

"Come up with something! Amy, this is the eighth-grade spring dance. You can't wait until the last minute and then just *come up* with something! You need time to coordinate your look."

"My what?"

"Your look. You know, your shoes, jewelry, makeup, hair. And you can't even think about those things until you get your dress." She sighed one of her long, deep sighs that meant she was at the end of her rope. "Everything depends on the dress."

Why is it that you always see a dress you would absolutely die for when you don't need one? But as soon as you're desperate for something, there's nothing there?

I looked through the rack again, hoping against hope. But it was no use. Every dress was either too flashy or too sophisticated or it made me look like an overgrown six-year-old.

"I give up," I said, raising my hands in the air. "I'm never going to find what I'm looking for."

"Exactly what are you looking for?"

"I have no idea. But I'll know it when I see it."

"You should try Lucilla's," she said. "That's where I got my dress. You'd find something fantastic there."

"I know, but my mom practically hyperventilates whenever I mention the name." Lucilla's was the chicest boutique in town. Every dress had a designer label. And every girl I knew had bought her dress there. Even Lisa.

"Won't she even let you look?"

"Nope. She says it's too expensive."

"But this is going to be the biggest night of our lives, and you've got an actual date!"

"Lis," I groaned. "I'm going with David."

"Well?"

"Well, I wouldn't exactly call it a date."

David Murdock and I had been friends since first grade. Oh, sure, there were times when I wanted to wring his neck, and other times when I had stopped talking to him. But when it came down to serious stuff—stuff like trust and respect—David was definitely someone I could always count on.

"We're just friends," I told Lisa. "We're buddies. Pals."

"Then explain *that*," she said, pointing to the bracelet I was wearing. I rubbed the silvery knots that circled my wrist and smiled. David had given it to me for Christmas.

"It's a friendship bracelet," I explained for

7

about the millionth time. "David and I are friends."

Lisa rolled her eyes.

"That's all it is!" I snapped.

"Look," she said, "I'm going to the dance with Marsha Wilson and a couple of the other girls, and you're going to the dance with David. You can *call* it anything you want, but I say it's a date."

I knew she thought I was holding something back from her, but I wasn't. David and I were friends. Just friends. That's all.

After sifting through one more rack of dresses, we went outside and parked ourselves on a bench to wait for Lisa's mother. My legs went dizzy with pleasure.

A half an hour later, we were still waiting. "I wonder what's keeping her," Lisa said, glancing at her watch.

I wiggled around on the bench. Now my behind was going numb. "She probably got caught in traffic. You know how bad it is on a Friday night."

"Yeah, but she made such a big deal about *us* being on time. 'Eight-fifteen. Don't be late,'" Lisa said, sounding more like her mother than her mother did.

I got up, walked around, then sat back down. "Are you sure she said eight-fifteen?" I asked.

"Positive," Lisa answered. "Eight-fifteen—in front of Sears."

"Sears?!?!" I shrieked.

We shot off the bench and looked at the JCPenney sign above our heads.

"I'm never going to live this down," Lisa said as we high-tailed it to the other side of the mall. "My mom's always on my back about not paying attention."

"Gee, I wonder why."

She threw me a dirty look.

Mrs. Howard's Dodge was wedged between a black van and a pickup truck. "Sorry, Mom," Lisa said as we jumped in the backseat.

Mrs. Howard glared at us through the rearview mirror. "I've been sitting here for a half an hour. Do you girls know what it's like to wait for someone for half an hour?"

"Yep," I said. Lisa jabbed me with her elbow. I guess Mrs. Howard didn't hear me.

"And now I have to stop for gas," she continued as we weaved into traffic. "I was going to stop on my way over, but I didn't want to be late."

Lisa looked at me and rolled her eyes. If she was expecting some sympathy from me, she was wasting her time. I was a little ticked off myself.

We pulled into a self-serve station. "I'm never

going to hear the end of this," Lisa moaned when her mother got out of the car. "Now every time I ask her to pick me up, she's going to hang this over my head."

Serves you right, I thought. My mind drifted back to the mall. I was wondering if I was ever going to find a dress, when Lisa gave me another jab.

"Hey, isn't that Carrie?" she asked.

"Where?"

"Over there," she said, pointing to a rusty, old pickup truck parked by another gas pump. The driver's side was empty. But there on the passenger's side was my sister Carrie.

"What's she doing here?" I asked. "Who's she with?"

"I don't know. She must have a date."

"A date? She's supposed to be at the library."

"Well . . . maybe someone's giving her a ride home."

I gave Lisa one of my *you've-got-to-be-kidding* looks. Home was on the other side of town— and so was the library. "Oh, sure, Lis. What are they doing? Taking the scenic route?"

"Well, you never know—" She stopped, her eyes almost popping out of her head. "Oh, no!"

I swung my eyes back to the truck just in time to see Nick Rafferty jump into the driver's seat. Carrie slid over until she was practically in his lap.

"Oh, gross," Lisa said. And she was right. Every town has a town sleaze—and Nick was ours. He was a sixteen-year-old freshman in high school (which tells you how smart the guy was) with greasy, black hair, dirty fingernails, and a smell like yesterday's garbage.

He turned on the engine and slipped an arm over Carrie's shoulders.

Lisa groaned.

I sank against the back of the seat, took some deep breaths, and tried not to barf.

"What is she doing with *him?*"

"I don't know," I said and took another deep breath as they drove away. "She's *supposed* to be at the library."

Chapter

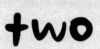

I had said I'd be home by nine o'clock. But when I walked in the door at twenty after, Mom and Dad were studying a book of wallpaper samples and didn't notice the time. Well, actually only Mom was studying it. Dad was just sitting there, looking absolutely bored with the whole thing.

"Oh, Amy. Come here," Mom said. "Tell me what you think of these."

I looked over her shoulder while she flipped through the book. She stopped and pointed to a sheet of green-and-gold striped paper.

"Nah," I said, shaking my head.

"Then how about this?" she asked, flipping ahead to another sheet. It was beige with huge, white swirls through it. Just looking at it made me dizzy.

"I still think we should paint," Dad said before I could answer. "Painting is easier, and

I still have those two cans of white in the basement."

"Paint's too boring," Mom said. "I want something with some personality to it."

Silently, I agreed with Dad. Our living room used to be white—perfectly good, boring white—and I liked it that way. Then last fall, Mom had decided to add some flair, and they painted it an ugly shade of mustard yellow. We all hated it.

Now, it looked as if we were going to try wallpaper. Green stripes or white swirls on stinky beige. *Great, just great.*

"Well, I'm not giving up," Mom said, snapping the book shut. "The perfect wallpaper is out there somewhere. And we're not stopping until we find it."

Dad groaned.

She ignored him and turned to me. "Did you find a dress?"

"Nope."

"You were gone all this time and you didn't find anything?"

"Nothing," I said, plopping on the reclining chair. "It's hopeless, Mom. There's just nothing out there." I leaned back and threw my arms over the chair. "I'm doomed."

Dad laughed a low, throaty laugh that told me he was amused by the whole thing.

I glared at him. Mom jabbed him with her elbow.

Dad picked up the remote control and zapped on the TV. Laughter from a prime-time sitcom filled the room.

"Don't mind him," Mom told me as she moved the book of samples to the coffee table. "And don't worry about the dress. I'll help you find something."

"When? The dance is only two weeks away, and Lisa and I already hit every store in the mall."

"How about the shops in town?"

"Like Lucilla's?"

"No."

"But, Mom—"

"No!"

"That's not fair! Everyone is wearing a dress from Lucilla's."

"Amy, we've been through this a dozen times. I'm not spending a fortune on one dress, and that's final! Besides, there are other boutiques in town. If you want to see what they have, I'll be happy to take you. What do you say? Do you want to look?"

"I don't know," I whined. "When would we go?"

"Tomorrow," she answered. "I want to take these wallpaper samples back and pick up

15

another book or two."

Dad groaned again.

She gave him another jab and continued, "Then we can do some serious shopping. We'll make a whole day of it. We'll do lunch."

Spending an entire Saturday with my mom has never been high on my list of fun things to do. Come to think of it, it's never been on the list at all. But it had been a while since we'd done anything together. And once she saw the junky dresses those other shops had, then maybe—just maybe—she'd change her mind about Lucilla's.

"Okay," I said. "Let's do it."

"Great," she said and shot me one of her *that's-my-girl* smiles.

I relaxed and tried to concentrate on the TV—but it was impossible. As soon as I recognized a show, Dad switched channels with the remote. Zap . . . zap, zap . . . zap. It was enough to drive you crazy.

Mom must have been having the same problem. She cleared her throat several times and when that didn't work, she grabbed the remote control out of his hand.

"Hey!" he yelled.

"You're giving me a headache," Mom complained.

"But it's a commercial," he answered, and

grabbed the control back. "I don't want to waste my time watching commercials."

She looked at me, rolled her eyes, then glanced at the clock. It was almost ten o'clock. She made a funny kind of sound—between a sigh and a groan—and jumped up and peeked through the blinds of the front window.

"I wonder what's keeping Carrie. She should have been home a half an hour ago."

I cringed. I knew what she was thinking. She was thinking that the library closed at nine o'clock like it usually did. But I remembered that today was Friday. And on Fridays, it closed at eight o'clock. Carrie should have been home an *hour* and a half ago.

I was dying to tell Mom what her older daughter was up to—but I didn't want to be a snitch. And I knew that just hearing Nick Rafferty's name would send her into one of her tailspins and it would take weeks for her to snap out of it.

I didn't need that.

Not now.

Not when I had a shot at getting her into Lucilla's. So, I sucked in my bottom lip and chewed on the fleshy part and prayed she wouldn't find out.

Mom returned to the sofa, flipped through the book of samples again, then snapped it shut. "Amy, the library *does* close at nine o'clock on Fridays, doesn't it?"

Uh-oh.

"I'm not sure," I said.

"I thought maybe it . . ."

Her voice trailed off and I zeroed in on the TV. It wasn't easy to pay attention since Dad was still zapping away like a man possessed.

Out of the corner of my eye, I saw Mom tapping her finger against her lips, the way she always did when she was trying to get her thoughts together.

Luckily, Carrie popped in before the pieces fell into place.

Mom sighed.

Dad stretched, laid the remote on his lap, and closed his eyes.

Carrie made a big point of dumping a pile of books on the coffee table and then carefully straightening them into a perfect stack.

"My, my," Mom said. "You've certainly had a busy night. Do you plan to read all those?"

"Sure," Carrie snapped. "Why do you think I brought them home?"

"Oh," Mom said, trying to laugh it off. "I guess it was a silly question.

Watching my mom with Carrie was like watching a tightrope walker in a strong wind. She swayed with every gust of wind and tried not to hit any slippery spots.

Carrie took off her jean jacket, threw it on a chair, and marched into the kitchen.

Mom's eyes were glued to that stack of books. From the other side of the sofa, Dad's heavy breathing told me he was out for the night. The TV was stuck on a boring documentary. *Great.*

Carrie returned with a can of soda and a bag of corn chips. She jammed the can in her back pocket, slipped the corner of the bag between her teeth, and scooped the books into her arms, hugging them to her chest.

I could tell that Mom was dying to say something. But Carrie was up the stairs before Mom could get any words out.

A few minutes later, I headed for Carrie's room. She was sitting on her bed, thumbing through the latest issue of *'TEEN* and popping corn chips in her mouth. Black-and-white posters of old-time movie stars covered her walls. And the books she had been so careful with downstairs were thrown all over her floor. I picked up the book closest to me and read the title aloud. *"The History of Modern Man.* You've got to be kidding."

"I'm into anthropology," she said between mouthfuls. "I think it's important to know where we came from."

"Yeah, right. Well, I know where you came from, and it wasn't the library."

"What are you talking about?" she asked.

"Carrie, I saw you with Nick Rafferty."

She jumped off the bed and shut the door. "You little sneak!"

"Me? A sneak? I was where I was supposed to be. But you weren't at the library."

"Yes, I was! I just didn't stay there the whole time, that's all. Did you squeal on me?"

"No, but—"

"You better not! I mean it, Amy. You say one word to Mom and I'm out of here. And this time I'm not coming back."

Normally, I would've told her what to do with her threat. Normally, it would've been the first thing out of my mouth. But things hadn't been normal in our family since last fall—since the day Mom and Dad painted our living room that ugly shade of yellow.

That was the day Carrie disappeared. The police listed her as a runaway, but she didn't really *run* away. She just packed her backpack and walked out the front door.

Poof, she was gone. And she stayed gone for five whole months. Mom and Dad went bonkers. When they weren't fighting with each other, they were fighting with me. Every privilege I had accumulated in my thirteen years was suddenly wiped out. No more going out on a school night. I had to be in by 9 p.m. on weekends. I could barely go to the bathroom without reporting in. Carrie had left—and I was punished.

It was the worst five months of my life.

And I wasn't about to let *that* happen again.

"But why Nick?" I asked. "Of all the guys you could hang out with, why him?"

"He's nice."

"Yeah, sure," I answered. I remembered the way he looked in the old pickup truck with his arm around Carrie.

"He is! You don't understand. You don't know—"

"I know a sleaze when I see one."

Her mouth twisted into a smirk and her eyes narrowed. "That's your problem," she hissed. "You judge everyone by what you see. That's about as deep as you can go, isn't it, Amy?"

"That's not true!"

"You're a snob," she snapped.

"And you're a liar! You weren't at the library all this time—and what I think about Nick doesn't change that!" I turned toward the door, but she grabbed my arm and yanked me back.

"I meant what I said, Amy. Don't tell Mom!"

Chapter

three

"**A**MY, exactly what kind of dress are you looking for?" Mom asked.

It was Saturday afternoon and we were standing in the tiny dressing room of Samantha's—*Mom's* favorite boutique.

"I don't know," I answered. "But it sure isn't this."

I hadn't even wanted to try the dress on. I hadn't wanted to try on all the others before it either—but Mom had insisted. She said that you couldn't tell by just looking at something on a rack. You had to see what it did for you, that dresses, like people, had personalities all their own.

It had sounded like good advice at the time. But as I stared in the mirror, I realized she was wrong. Some dresses aren't worth the bother—sometimes you can tell just by looking. *And this is one of those dresses,* I thought.

The color wasn't bad, and it was just the right length, and it did fit perfectly. But it made me stick out in places I didn't want to stick out in. And it wasn't from Lucilla's.

"What's wrong with it?" Mom asked.

"It's the ruffles. I'm just not a ruffle person, Mom."

She shook her head. "You're not a ruffle person. You're not a lace person. You don't like bows. You don't like beads. Sequins are out. Green isn't your color." She went on and on.

"But, Mom," I said the second she paused to catch her breath. "Look at this dress. I mean, take a good look at it. Would *you* wear something like this?"

Her eyes darted from my head to my toes, and I spun around so she could get the entire effect. "Well, I guess the ruffles are a little much, and—"

The dressing room door swung open before she could finish, and a saleslady swooshed in. That was the one thing I hated about these stores. They barged in on you whenever they felt like it. You could be standing there stark naked, but did they care? Noooo.

"Oh, dah-ling," the lady gushed. "You look so bea-u-ti-ful! That dress was definitely made with you in mind."

Oh, brother.

Samantha's was our last stop. I begged Mom to take me to Lucilla's. I begged and pleaded and whined like I never whined before, but it was no use. She wouldn't budge.

"Can't we just go in and look?" I asked as we headed for the car.

"No!"

"But, Mom—"

"You're not getting a dress from Lucilla's, Amy. Why can't you get that through your head?"

We drove home in silence.

I helped Mom lug the packages (of course, she had found some things *she* liked for *herself*) and more wallpaper samples into the house. Dad was sprawled on the floor, rewiring a lamp, while a baseball game blared from the TV.

"Where's Carrie?" Mom asked as soon as she saw him.

"Over at Melanie's."

I froze. Hearing Melanie's name always made me stop in my tracks. It was nothing personal against Melanie—she was Carrie's best friend. But that's where we thought Carrie was going the day she disappeared.

Carrie and Melanie usually spent their weekends together. So when Carrie walked out the door that Saturday in late October, no one had asked her where she was going. We didn't have to. We all thought we knew the answer. It wasn't until later that evening, when Carrie didn't come home for supper, that we realized something was wrong.

That was when my life started falling apart.

"Are you sure she's at Melanie's?" Mom asked, and I knew she was thinking the same thing I was. "Did she say that was where she was going? Or are you just assuming—"

"She said it," Dad snapped.

Mom flinched.

My stomach flip-flopped the way it always did when I smelled a fight in the air.

"And I didn't even have to ask her," he continued with a hint of pride in his voice. "She told me on her own. And she said she'd be home in time for supper."

"And what time is that, Peter? Do you know the exact hour? And what time did she leave? How long has she been gone? Did you call Melanie's house to see if she was really there?"

The questions flew from her mouth so fast I had trouble keeping up with them.

Dad didn't even try. "You can't put a leash on her, Elizabeth! She's fifteen years old. You're just going to have to trust her."

I wanted to tell him that he was wrong, that trusting Carrie was the last thing in the world anyone should do.

I wanted to tell them about Nick Rafferty and the library. The words were sitting right there on the tip on my tongue. But Carrie's threat was ringing in my ears, and I couldn't spit the words out.

Mom didn't say anything either. She gathered her packages and headed for the stairs, worry etched in her face.

I just stood there, wishing Carrie would come home so everyone could relax.

"Oh, Amy," Dad said, "I almost forgot. Lisa called. She wants you to call her back."

I stepped over a lamp shade and a coil of electrical wires, went into the kitchen, and picked up the phone. Lisa's line was busy.

I tried three more times.

Busy, busy, busy.

I slammed down the receiver, then picked it up and dialed a different number.

Melanie answered on the first ring.

"Hey, Mel, it's Amy. Could I speak to Carrie for a minute?"

"Sorry, she's not here."

"Oh, you mean she left already?"

"No, she hasn't been here, Amy. I haven't seen her all day."

Chapter
four

MOM had whipped up some kind of chicken casserole for supper and we were just sitting down to eat when Carrie came home.

Mom's eyes lit up.

Dad had *I told you so* written all over his face.

I had to sit on my hands to keep from strangling my sister. I'd just spent hours agonizing over whether or not to tell my parents that she wasn't at Melanie's, hours wondering if she'd disappeared again. Hours worrying about what would happen if I made the wrong decision. I had worried about it so long that it had gotten to be supper time before I decided anything.

All that time, all that energy, and for what? Nothing, that's what! Carrie was just busy being Carrie.

"How's Melanie?" Mom asked.

"Okay, I guess," Carrie answered with a shrug.

I picked mushrooms out of the casserole on my plate and piled them on the side. "What did the two of you do all day?"

"Nothing much."

"Did you stay at Melanie's house the whole time or did you—"

"What are you doing, Mom? Writing a book?"

Mom flinched.

Dad grabbed a roll and swabbed it with butter. I searched for more mushrooms.

"I'm just making conversation," Mom explained.

"No, you're not," Carrie snapped. "You're giving me the third degree."

"I am not!"

"You are! I promised that every time I went out I'd tell you where I was going and who I'd be with, and I've kept that promise. But you can't stop digging, can you?"

"I was just making conversation," Mom repeated.

"Elizabeth," Dad said, his fork poised in midair, "maybe you should just change the subject."

Mom didn't tackle another subject, and

neither did anyone else. We ate in silence. When we were finished, everyone helped clear the table, and Carrie and I were left with the dishes. She washed; I dried.

"So," I said, swinging the dish towel around my arm, "how's Nick?"

"What do you mean, 'how's Nick?'"

"You weren't at Melanie's today, Carrie. I called her house and she said she hadn't seen you all day."

"You little sneak!" she hissed. "You've been checking up on me!"

"I wasn't checking up on you!" I told Carrie about Mom being upset when we came home from shopping, and how she and Dad were on the verge of a fight, and how I had called Melanie's, hoping to convince her to come home early so things would calm down.

I told her all that while she threw clean silverware all over the draining board.

"Don't give me that baloney," she said. "First of all, Mom and Dad don't fight."

"What?! Where have you been for the past fifteen years? They fight all the time."

"No, they don't," she answered. "You just saw them. Mom gets started on something, then Dad opens his mouth and Mom gets quiet. That's the way it is. That's the way it's always been."

"That doesn't mean they're not fighting! Mom cries—she cries a lot. Sometimes I hear her before I fall asleep at night."

Carrie gave me a "so what" kind of shrug and threw more silverware my way.

"You don't care, do you? You don't care about any of us."

"This doesn't have anything to do with caring," she said, throwing the last fork on the drainer. "It has to do with respect. I respect their privacy and I expect them to respect mine. Understand?"

I didn't say anything.

"And that goes for you, too, Miss Busy-Body." She leaned toward me until we were nose-to-nose. "Remember—I can take care of myself."

◆ ◆ ◆ ◆

"You're kidding," Lisa shrieked over the phone a few hours later. "You mean to tell me your parents still don't know she wasn't at Melanie's? You mean they don't even suspect anything?"

"That's exactly what I mean," I whispered. I was using the phone in my parents' bedroom for privacy. But I kept my voice real low and peeked into the hall every few minutes to make sure no one was lurking around. "And they don't know about last night either," I continued.

"You're not going to tell on her, are you?"

"I can't." I peeked into the hall again then collapsed on the bed and told her about Carrie's threat to leave.

"You couldn't tell on her anyway," she said.

"Why not?"

"Because that would make you a snitch."

"I know, but—"

"But nothing. Amy, there's nothing worse than being a snitch."

I knew she was right. But something told me that this was different. Something told me that what Carrie was doing was worse than being a snitch.

If only she hadn't made that threat.

"Where is she now?" Lisa asked.

"Downstairs." I rolled off the bed and checked the hall. All clear. "She's trying to get on Mom's good side by helping her pick out wallpaper for the living room."

"That's great!"

"Huh? What do you mean?"

"It's great you're getting new wallpaper. No offense, Amy, but those mustard-colored walls are the pits. Every time I'm in your house, I get this awful craving for a hot dog."

"That's cute, Lis. Real cute."

We stayed on that topic for a few minutes, then switched to the upcoming dance. I told her about my shopping trip with Mom and how we hit every store in town, but I still didn't have a dress to wear.

"Did you go to Lucilla's?"

"No."

"Amy, you *have* to go to Lucilla's. You just *have* to."

When I hung up, I went downstairs. Mom and Carrie were in the dining room with wall-paper samples spread all over the table.

"Amy, look at this," Mom said, pushing an open book in my direction. "Do you like it?"

I glanced at a sheet of tiny, colored flowers on a white background and sighed.

"You don't like it?" Mom asked.

It wasn't that I didn't like it. It was that I didn't care. I had a lot of important things on my mind—and wallpaper *wasn't* one of them.

"It's okay," I said and sighed again.

"It's not just okay," Carrie said. "It's perfect. The white background will make the living room look larger. And look at the colors in these flowers. They match our sofa, carpet, and curtains."

Mom was nodding her head.

"This pattern," Carrie continued, tapping on the open book while her eyes darted between me and Mom, "will harmonize the entire room without overpowering it. *And* if you ever decide to change the curtains or anything, you'll have a lot of different colors to choose from."

Carrie was one of those people who always sounded like she knew what she was talking about. She was good at it. Real good. Hey, she had me convinced. I was ready to order a hundred rolls and I didn't even care about the stupid wallpaper!

Mom smiled. "I think you're right. I think this is the one I've been looking for."

"You'll love it, Mom," Carrie said. "Trust me."

Ha!

"Then it's settled," Mom said. "I'll have your father measure the living room and I'll place the order on Monday." Then she turned to me and said, "The next thing we have to do is find a dress for that dance."

"You *still* didn't find a dress?" Carrie asked.

"Nope. And I'm never going to find one . . . unless I can go to Lucilla's."

"No," Mom said.

"That's not fair," I argued. "All the kids are getting their dresses at Lucilla's. Why do you always make me the oddball?"

"Why do you always have to follow the crowd?" she shot back. "This is an eighth-grade dance, Amy. It's not the senior prom. I'm not about to spend a fortune on a dress you'll probably outgrow by the end of the summer."

"But, Mom—"

"No!"

◆ ◆ ◆ ◆

Later that night, Carrie dragged me into her room and closed the door. "I've got the answer to your problem," she said as she pulled a dress from the back of her closet. It was covered with a filmy white plastic bag that had *Lucilla's* stamped across the front in fancy script. She lifted the bag and showed me the most gorgeous dress I'd ever seen.

I'd been tearing my brains out looking for the perfect dress, and it had been right here the whole time—right here in Carrie's closet! And I'd never seen it before.

Wait a minute, I thought before I got too excited. *Wait one minute.* "Where'd you get it?" I asked her.

"I borrowed it."

"From whom?"

"Beats me," she answered. "I've had it for so long, I can't remember."

"You can't remember!"

"Look, don't make such a big deal out of it. If it was that important, whoever I borrowed it from would have asked for it back by now, wouldn't she?"

"Carrie, you were gone for five months. How *could* someone ask for it back?"

She ignored the question and handed me the dress. "Here," she said. "Try it on. If it fits, you can wear it."

"I don't know if I should."

"But it's perfect."

I know, I thought. *That's the problem. It's too perfect.* Having a dress from Lucilla's just fall into my hands seemed too good to be true. And my dad always said that if something seemed too good to be true, it probably was.

That's all I could think of as Carrie dangled the dress in front of me. I could see the designer label, and I couldn't imagine how anyone could just lose track of a dress like that. If it was mine, I'd post a guard at my closet door.

"Oh, forget it," Carrie said. "I thought I was doing you a favor but . . ." She shrugged and started to put the dress away. In another minute it would be gone. Out of my sight. Lost forever.

"Wait!" I said. "I guess there's no harm in trying it on."

I was wrong. Trying it on was a *big* mistake.

It not only looked perfect and fit perfect—it *felt* perfect. It settled over my body like a breath of air, and it moved when I moved. It was like wearing a breeze. A soft, cool, light breeze.

"I don't believe this," I said, swirling in front of the mirror while Carrie watched from the bed. "The kids are going to flip when they see me in this."

"I told you it was perfect," she said.

I couldn't argue with that. And I knew I wanted to wear the dress. I wanted it so badly, I knew I'd never be happy with anything else. But it wasn't mine and it wasn't Carrie's. I didn't even know where it came from.

"Could you find out whose it is?" I asked her. "I'd feel better if the owner said it was okay to wear it."

"I'm telling you it's okay. That's all you need."

I thought about it while I changed back into my jeans and hung the dress back on its hanger. By the time I had it tucked back in its bag, I knew I couldn't part with it.

"Okay," I said. "I'll wear it, but only because you said it was all right."

"No sweat. I'll take full responsibility."

I laid the dress over my arm and kept it away from my body so I wouldn't crush a single thread.

"Amy, one more thing. Don't tell Mom

where you got it."

"What?!"

"You heard me. Don't tell Mom."

"Why not?"

"Because she'll freak out, that's why. I've had that dress forever, and if Mom sees that designer label, she'll be knocking on every door in town until she finds out whose it is. And you won't have a dress to wear."

"But what am I supposed to tell her?"

"Just tell her you borrowed it."

"Who would lend me a dress like this?"

"How about Lisa?"

"Carrie, Lisa has *one* dress from Lucilla's and she's wearing it to the dance."

"Mom doesn't know that. Tell her Lisa has a couple of designer dresses."

"I-I don't know, Carrie. I don't like lying."

"You're not lying. You're bending the truth. You borrowed the dress, right? That's all that counts. That's all Mom has to know."

"But I don't like it. I—"

"Don't be stupid. You'll never find another dress like that, never in a million years."

Chapter

five

SUNDAY arrived with a fresh morning face. Except for a few fluffy clouds, the sky was crystal clear. Every few minutes my bedroom curtains puffed themselves with springtime air.

It was a hard day to ignore. I shifted sideways at my desk, so my back was to the window, and tried to concentrate on my social studies project. The fact was, I had a major report due first thing Monday morning, and I didn't have a word of it written.

It took a while for me to block out the springtime weather. But then my mind skipped right over my report and landed on the dress that was now hanging in *my* closet.

Should I wear it or shouldn't I?

Should I tell Mom the truth or should I take Carrie's advice? I hated the idea of lying to Mom, but she didn't understand how important this dance was. I had to wear a dress from Lucilla's. I just had to.

"Sure," Lisa said when I told her about the dress and Carrie's plan to say I had borrowed it from her.

It was Monday morning and I had her cornered at her locker while I explained the situation. I had expected some kind of argument—a couple of "I don't knows", a few "Keep me out of its", and some "Are you crazys?" thrown in for good measure. But she didn't say any of those things. She didn't even blink an eye. She just said, "Sure."

"Lis, are you all right?"

"I'm fine," she said, throwing a book into her locker. "Just fine."

"You'll back up my story?"

"Sure."

"Lis, do you think this will work? Do you think my mom will believe that you have a *couple* of designer dresses?"

"She doesn't have to believe it," she answered. "I'm not going to the dance, so you can just tell her I lent you—"

"Whoa! Wait a minute! What do you mean you're not going to the dance? I thought you and Marsha—"

"Marsha has a date."

"You're kidding!"

"Nope. Denny Houser asked her."

"Denny Houser! Denny Houser, the class geek?"

"That's the one. He called her Saturday night, and she called me yesterday. I couldn't believe it."

I couldn't believe it either. Denny didn't speak English; he spoke computers. His entire vocabulary consisted of words like *modem, floppy disk,* and *menu.*

"That's going to be weird," I said to Lis as we headed for our homeroom. And the more I thought about it, the weirder it got. "What are they going to talk about? Marsha doesn't know her hardware from her software."

"I know, but Denny's had a crush on her ever since she asked him a question in computer science class."

"What did she ask him?"

"She asked, 'How do you turn this thing on?' Then she batted her eyes and the rest, as they say, is history."

"Does Marsha have a crush on him?"

"No, I don't think so. That's what really has me ticked off. We made plans to go to the dance together. It was all set. I even bought my dress—then she turns around and does *this* at the last minute. And she doesn't even like the guy!"

"Then why is she going with him?" I wondered.

"Because *everyone* who's going has a date."

"Not *everyone*. What about Patty and Monica and Helen? I thought you and Marsha were going to meet them there."

"We were," Lisa said. "But now Patty's not going either, and Monica got a date, and Helen asked her cousin to —oops!" She frowned and shook her head. "I wasn't supposed to say that," she whispered. "You won't tell anyone, will you? She doesn't want anyone to know it's her cousin."

"Lis, who would I tell? By the time I find something out, the rest of the school already knows about it."

"Well, they don't know about this. So you have to promise."

"My lips are sealed. But, Lis, this doesn't mean you can't go to the dance."

"I'm not going to go by myself, Amy."

"You won't have to. There's got to be someone else you can hook up with."

"Nope. The word's out. It's couples only," she said.

My head was spinning. How could it all change so fast? On Friday, everything was set. Plans were planned, arrangements were made, dresses were bought (except for mine,

44

of course). And now—*whammo*—Lisa wasn't going. One weekend, that's all it took. One weekend—and a guy named Denny Houser.

◆ ◆ ◆ ◆

At lunchtime, Marsha didn't sit with us like she usually did. She sat with Denny.

"That's it!" Lisa said as she stabbed a fork into her food. "I never want to hear Marsha Wilson's name again. Never—ever—again!"

"But maybe she really likes Denny," I said. "Maybe she just doesn't want to admit it."

"Oh, come on!"

Okay, so that idea was a little far-fetched. But Marsha wasn't the only one who had pulled up roots and moved on. Monica was sitting with Joel Preston, and Patty and Helen were at opposite ends of a table, shooting daggers at each other. Even David Murdock wasn't sitting where he usually—

Wait a minute. Where the heck was he?

I swiveled around and searched the tables behind me.

"Hey, Phillips."

I jumped and swiveled back all at the same time. David had slipped into Marsha's empty spot. His tray was piled high with double servings of everything. "Hey, Murdock! Don't

45

sneak up on me like that!"

"I wasn't sneaking. You weren't paying attention," he said with a smile that made me melt. Sometimes when I looked at him, I couldn't believe that he was the same scrawny, blond-haired kid I grew up with. He was a half a head taller than I was now, and his blond hair was turning golden brown. And he had two of the deepest dimples I'd ever seen.

I often wondered if I looked any different to him.

"I got them," he said as he opened his carton of milk.

"Got what?"

"The tickets for the dance. They went on sale this morning, and I was the first one in line."

He was beaming with pride, waiting for a pat on the back. But with Lisa sitting right next to me, I didn't want to talk about the dance. So I said, "That's nice," and tried to change the subject. "Did you get your social studies project done on time?"

"Oh, I got that done weeks ago," he said. *Wouldn't you know it?* "We still have to figure out how we're going to get there, you know."

"Get where?"

"The dance! Do you think your mom or dad would mind—"

"David, let's talk about this later."

"It's okay," Lisa said. "You can talk about the dance. Just pretend I'm not here."

David looked at Lisa, then me, then at Lisa again.

"She's not going to the dance," I explained. Then I told him about Marsha and Denny while Lisa threw in words like *back-stabbed* and *two-timing fink*. When she ran out of words, David asked her to come with us.

I almost choked on my milk.

Lisa said, "No way."

"Why not?" David asked. "The three of us have gone places before."

"This is different," she said. "This is couples only."

"That doesn't matter," he said and he told her to think about it.

Lisa said, "Thanks, but there's nothing to think about."

"You'll change your mind," David said. "I know Amy will talk you into it."

Wanna bet? I thought.

I hated myself for feeling that way, but I couldn't help it. My head told me that having Lisa come with us was the perfect solution. But the rest of me wasn't listening.

David was waiting for me after school. His grandmother lived a few blocks away from me. He had been living with her since he was three years old, when his parents were killed in a car accident.

We usually walked home together while Lisa took the bus. The air had that spring-time sweetness that made you wish you could stay outside forever.

"Did you have any luck?" he asked as we weaved through a maze of double-parked cars in front of the school.

"With what?"

"With Lisa. Is she coming to the dance with us?"

I shook my head.

"Well, at least we tried."

My cheeks got hot. I wanted Lisa to go to the dance. But I didn't want to be part of a threesome. There had to be another answer to this problem. There just had to be.

We talked about the dance and who was going with whom, and then he asked, "How's Carrie doing these days?"

Carrie. Another problem to be solved.

I must have been wearing that thought on my face, because David looked at me and said, "That bad, huh?"

I nodded. "She's hanging around with Nick

Rafferty. Lisa and I saw them together on Friday night. She was supposed to be at the library. And then on Saturday, she told Dad she was going to Melanie's. But when I called, Melanie said she hadn't seen her all day. So, I guess she was with Nick again."

"How'd she ever get hooked up with him?"

"I don't know," I groaned. "I don't even know if I want to know."

"Your parents must've hit the roof when they heard about that."

"They don't know."

"You didn't tell them?"

"No. I was going to, but then Carrie said if I squealed on her, she'd run away again— and this time she wouldn't come back."

"And you believed her?"

"Sure I believed her."

He looked at me like I was crazy—like I was the one with the problem.

"She did it before," I yelled. "Remember? She disappeared for five whole months and we didn't know if she was dead or alive!" My voice cracked. *Dead or alive.* Just thinking about it made me want to cry. "It was horrible, Murdock! Do you hear me? Horrible! And I never want to go through that again!"

My eyes filled with tears. I spun around so he wouldn't see and ran across the street. I wanted to get away from him . . . away from the memories . . . away from the gut-wrenching fear that it could all happen again.

"Phillips!" He was right behind me, his sneakers pounding the sidewalk, his voice ringing in my ears.

I tried to run faster, but I couldn't do it. I just couldn't do it.

He grabbed my arm and yanked me back so hard, I fell against him. I tried to push away, but he wrapped his arms around me and pulled me closer. I sobbed into his chest, soaking his shirt while he tightened his grip.

We walked home that way.

Neither of us said a word.

There was nothing left to say.

Chapter

Six

CARRIE couldn't believe my luck when I told her that Lisa wasn't going to the dance.

"What a break!" she said, plopping on my bed while I tried to finish my math homework. "Now your story will make even more sense than it did before. She's lending you her one and only dress from Lucilla's because she changed her mind about the dance. It's the perfect explanation. You are so lucky!"

I didn't feel lucky. I felt like a traitor. David had come up with an answer to Lisa's problem and I hadn't done a thing about it. And to top it all off, I let him think I had.

But when I told Carrie about it, she just laughed. "David Murdock's a jerk," she said.

"He is not!"

"He is. Any guy who would even think about asking two girls to a dance is a—"

"He was being nice," I snapped before she

could finish. "Lisa's his friend, too."

"Yeah, but you're his girlfriend."

"I am not! I'm just a friend. Period."

"Then why didn't you try to talk Lisa into going with you?" she asked with a smirk.

"Because I would have been wasting my time. She'd never go along with that idea. It's couples only."

"Oh, come on, Amy. You didn't ask her because you were afraid she'd say yes."

"That's not true!" I yelled, jamming my pencil down so hard I broke the point.

She pushed herself off my bed and laughed her way out of my room.

After I muddled through my math and tried to read some social studies, I threw my books in the corner and opened my closet.

The dress was still there.

It was so perfect—and I now had the perfect story to hand to Mom. But I still wasn't sure I should go through with it. What if something happened to it? What if I spilled something on it and ruined it forever? What if Mom found out I lied? Or even worse, what if she found out at the last minute, and I was left with nothing to wear to the dance?

It's not worth it, I told myself. *You'll be a nervous wreck. It's not worth the aggravation.*

But Carrie was right. I'd never find another

dress like it. Never in a million years.

I pulled the dress out of my closet and tried it on again. Then I hit the button on my radio and my favorite station blasted through my room. It was playing a song about feeling special, feeling classy. I swayed and twirled to the music and every time I caught sight of myself in the mirror, I knew the singer was singing it just for me.

That's how the dress made me feel. Classy. Special. Different from anyone else. I didn't want the song to end. But it did—right in the middle of a verse. I spun around and Mom was standing by my radio, her hand still on the button.

"Amy, where did you get that dress?"

I couldn't talk. I couldn't even think.

"Answer me, Amy! Where did you get that dress?"

"From Lisa."

There, I'd said it—and it was all Mom's fault. She shouldn't have sneaked up on me.

"Lisa?"

"Yeah. Sh-she bought it for the dance—but now she's not going. So she said I could borrow it. She gave it to me after school."

"Why isn't she going?"

I told her about Marsha and Denny and how everyone had a date. When I was finished, she cocked her head to the side and said, "I don't know, honey. That's a very expensive dress, and what if Lisa changes her mind? You both can't wear it."

"She won't change her mind, Mom. And I know it's expensive. But that's why she wants me to wear it—so it won't go to waste." That last part had to convince her. She was always complaining about things going to waste.

But she just stood there, shaking her head while my hands got clammy.

"I don't know," she repeated with a sigh.

"Aw, come on, Mom, pleeease."

"Well, it certainly is pretty . . ."

Yes, yes, yes.

". . . and I guess if her mother said it was okay—"

"She did." What else was I going to say?

"Then I guess it's all right. But if Lisa changes her mind, you have to give it back to her. No arguments."

The dress was mine! One problem solved. One decision made. I couldn't believe how easy it had been.

She was on her way out the door when she suddenly stopped and said, "That's funny."

"What?" I asked, holding my breath.

"I didn't think you and Lisa were the same size."

My stomach turned upside down. I hadn't thought of that. Mom was right. We weren't the same size. We couldn't fit in each other's clothes.

She shook her head again and said, "I guess looks are deceiving." And then she left.

I tackled Lisa first thing Tuesday morning. We had to get our stories straight. She listened and nodded and agreed with everything I said. But I could tell her heart wasn't in it. She was still in the dumps about Marsha and Denny. So even though I was dying to tell her all about the dress, I decided to keep my mouth shut before I sent her into a major depression. I didn't want her to feel worse than she already did.

David had baseball practice after school, so I ended up on the bus with Lisa. We talked about everything but the dance. When Marsha waved from across the aisle, Lisa turned her head. I waved back and hoped that Lisa didn't see.

When I got home, the house was empty. Mom and Dad were still at work, but Carrie was supposed to be there. Because she had missed most of her sophomore year at school when she left home, she was going to have to start all over again in September. In the meantime, she was supposed to be at home, helping with the housework.

But from the looks of things, she hadn't been home all day. There was an empty mug sitting on the coffee table, right where Dad had left it that morning. Yesterday's newspaper was scattered all over the floor. The kitchen was even worse. The dishes were piled in the sink, and there were crumbs all over the table.

There was a note hanging on the refrigerator door.

Amy,

Clean up for me, okay? I owe you one.

Carrie

I grabbed it and threw it in the garbage. I told myself not to do it. I told myself it was crazy to cover for her. She was a sneak and a liar and she deserved to get caught. I kept telling myself that while I scrubbed dried syrup off the breakfast dishes, cleaned the table, and straightened the living room. When I was finished, I popped open a can of soda and was planning the perfect murder when the phone rang.

It was Carrie.

"Where are you?" I screamed.

She ignored my question and said, "I'm going to be late. You'll have to cover for me."

"What?!"

"Tell Mom I'm at Melanie's and that I'm

staying for supper. Tell her I'll be home around—"

"No!"

"What do you mean, no?"

"I'm not covering for you, Carrie. I did your work, but I'm not going to lie for you, too."

"Do you like the dress?" she asked in a voice that made me go numb.

"W-what?"

"Mom told me all about it after you left for school this morning," she continued. "She told me that Lisa isn't going to the dance and that she lent you her dress."

"So?"

"So, you did a great job, Amy. Mom bought the whole story. She believed every word of it, and she couldn't be happier. You have the dress of your dreams, and she doesn't have to shell out any money. It would be a shame to ruin it all now."

"What are you getting at, Carrie?"

"If you don't cover for me, I'm going to tell Mom you lied about the dress."

"You wouldn't!"

"Want to try me?"

"You're bluffing, Carrie. If you tell Mom I lied then I'll have to tell her where that dress really came from."

"So what? I'll end up making some phone

calls to try to remember where it came from. Big deal. But you'll be out one designer dress. And you know how upset Mom gets about lying. She'll probably ground you so long, you'll end up missing the dance."

"I can't believe you'd be so mean."

"Poor David," she went on. "He'll be so disappointed. But I guess he could ask Lisa to go with him. After all, she doesn't have a date and it is couples—"

I slammed the phone down.

◆ ◆ ◆ ◆

Mom actually smiled when I told her Carrie was having supper with Melanie. "I'm glad she hasn't lost any of her friends," she said as she kicked her shoes off and flipped through the mail. "I was afraid she'd have to start all over when she came home, but she just picked up where she left off."

You don't know how right you are, I thought.

Chapter

seven

DAVID thought I was crazy when I told him how I had covered for Carrie. He said it was the stupidest thing I had ever done.

And he was right. I *was* crazy and stupid—crazy and stupid for telling him about it. Of course, he didn't know why I had covered for Carrie. He didn't know about the dress and I couldn't tell him about it. I wanted it to be a surprise. So I just listened while we walked home from school.

It was Wednesday. Another week and a half and I'd slip into that dress and have the best night of my life. And then it would be over. No more worry about the dance or the dress or Lisa—and Carrie could tell Mom anything she wanted to. It wouldn't matter anymore.

"If you *really* cared about Carrie, you'd tell," David said as we rounded a corner.

I stopped and glared at him. I could ignore a lot of the things he said, but I couldn't let that one slip by. "What do you mean, if I *really* cared? Why do you think I'm doing this? I'm trying to keep my family together!"

He stopped and stood right in front of me. "But Nick's bad news, Amy. Real bad news. And if Carrie was my sister, I'd do everything I could to make sure she stayed away from him."

"But I *can't* say anything!" I screamed. "I told you what she said. Weren't you listening?"

"Yeah, but what if she's bluffing?"

"And what if she isn't? She said that this time she'd never come back. That means she'd be gone forever. Forever, Murdock! Do you know how long forever is?" My throat tightened and my eyes burned. I stepped around him and started walking so he wouldn't see that I was about to cry.

But he wouldn't let up. He fell into step next to me and said, "I know you're scared, Amy. But keeping your mouth shut isn't going to help. The more time she spends with Nick, the more trouble she's going to get into. He's probably got her hooked on something already."

"Hooked? What do you mean hooked? Hooked on what?"

"Drugs," he said.

"How did drugs get into this?"

"Come on, Amy, you know Nick. The guy's a walking billboard for the stuff."

"I don't know anything about any drugs. And besides, Carrie would never do that. She's not that stupid."

"Isn't she?"

"You *want* her to run away again, don't you?" I said, stepping in front of him. "You always hated her. When she ran away before, you called her a monster."

"*I* didn't call her a monster. *You* called her a monster. I just agreed with you."

"Aw, forget it, Murdock. Just forget it," I yelled and ran away.

But this time he didn't follow.

This time I was on my own.

◆ ◆ ◆ ◆

I used to think that life was simple. That's the way my parents and teachers made it seem.

"Just tell the truth," they said.

They made it sound so easy. They made it sound like the world was divided into black and white, and all you had to do was choose the right color.

But if I told on Carrie, I'd lose her forever.

David might think she was bluffing, but I knew she wasn't. Carrie said a lot of things she didn't really mean. But if you crossed her, she'd go through with something just to get even. That's the way she was. That's how she operated.

And if I *didn't* tell on her, she might end up in a whole lot of trouble.

The problem was, Carrie wasn't black or white. She was gray. A swirling, massive, shade of gray.

And I didn't know what to do with gray. What are you supposed to do with gray?

I was so wrapped up in that question that when Mr. Williams called me later that night, it took me a few minutes to figure out who he was. But as soon as he mentioned the word *play*, it all clicked into place.

He was the high school drama teacher who had directed our school play a few months ago. Lisa had talked me into going to the audition and I ended up with a great part. And you know what? Mr. Williams told me I had a lot of talent.

Me, Amy Phillips! Talented!

And now he was telling me again. "You were remarkable, Amy," he said. "Simply remarkable."

Jelly-kneed, I slid down the kitchen wall and plopped on the floor.

"And that's why I thought of you right away," he said.

Remarkable. That's what he had said. *Simply remarkable.* I'd heard him with my own two ears. Well, okay, one ear—and I was turning to mush.

"The Community Theater is doing *West Side Story* this summer," he continued, "and I thought it would be a great experience for you. Are you interested?"

"Oh . . . gee . . . I don't know. I haven't thought about it." Actually, I hadn't even known about it, and my heart was still bouncing around because of that *remarkable* word he had thrown in my ear. I couldn't think.

"Would you consider it?" he asked.

"Yeah, sure." *Why not?*

He told me about the character he thought I should audition for, and then he gave me a short run-down on the story line. The more he talked, the more excited I got.

Another play, another character—another chance to be someone else. I'd forgotten how great that felt. When he was finished, I told him I'd do it.

"Great!" he said, like he really meant it. "I'll get you a copy of the script. In the meantime, you can see the movie on tape. Do you have a VCR?"

I said, "Yes," and that made him even happier. "I'm really looking forward to working with you again, Amy."

Aw, shucks.

"I'll get that script to you as soon as I can. If you have any questions about it, give me a call. If I don't hear from you, I'll see you next Friday at the community center. Seven o'clock sharp."

"Friday? You mean *this* Friday?"

"No, next Friday. A week and a half from now." I couldn't answer. I couldn't say a word. I couldn't even move. Even when he said goodbye and hung up and the dial tone was buzzing away in my ear, I was still sitting there with the phone in my hand.

◆ ◆ ◆ ◆

"What am I going to do, Mom?" I asked, following her through the hall and into the bathroom. "The dance is next Friday and so is the audition. I told Mr. Williams I'd be there. But I don't want to miss the dance. What am I going to do?"

"Honey, you'll just have to choose one. You can't be in two places at the same time." She opened the linen closet and groaned. "Look at this mess," she said and handed me the pile of freshly folded towels she had in her arms. I peeked over her shoulder. The shelves were clogged with crumpled sheets and balled-up towels. "Carrie's supposed to be helping me with the housework," she said as she straightened the linens. "But I swear, all she's doing is making more work for me. What does that girl do all day?"

No, please, not now. I can't handle Carrie now, I thought. But luckily, Mom wasn't expecting an answer.

"I told her to do the laundry today," she continued, "and what does she do? She dumps four loads of clean wash on my bed. And when I complained about it, she said, 'You didn't tell me I had to put it away.'"

Sounds like the Carrie I know.

"Can you believe that? I didn't tell her she had to put it away."

I waited until she cleared a spot for the towels then I handed them to her and took off before she roped me into folding that mountain of laundry that was still on her bed.

I found Dad in the kitchen with Carrie. They were polishing off a coconut cream pie that Mom had brought home. I joined them at the table and spilled out my problem.

"What am I going to do, Dad?" It seemed as if I'd been asking that question, in one way or another, forever. But he wasn't any help either. In fact, he was worse than Mom. He made a speech about how we have to make certain choices in life, about how no one can make those decisions for us, and how we never know if it's the right decision until after we've made it and we're living with the results.

He went on and on while Carrie and I shot *is-he-ever-going-to-stop?* looks at each other across the table.

When he finally ran out of things to say, I trudged upstairs and flopped on my bed. A few minutes later, Carrie came up. She peered down the hall then dashed in my room and closed the door.

"What's wrong?" I asked.

"Shhh," she said. "I don't want Mom to know I'm in here. She's still folding clothes."

"You knew you were supposed to do that. It's part of the job."

"I know, but I didn't have time. I was running late."

Late for what? I wondered, but I didn't ask. I didn't want to know. It was easier not knowing.

She walked around to the other side of my bed and sat on the floor. "So what are you going to do about the dance?"

"I don't know," I moaned, flipping on my stomach so I could see her. "I want to do both, and it's just not fair. There are 365 days in the year and the two most important things in my life are crowded into the same spot."

"You have to think this thing through," she said, crossing her legs Indian-style. "And to do that, you have to look at the whole picture. You're not just deciding between a dance or an audition, you know. You're choosing between a night of bliss and a summer of excitement."

"Huh?"

"If you choose the dance," she explained, "you'll have a good time for a couple of hours then it'll be over and you'll be bored all summer. But if you choose the audition, you're going to miss the greatest night of your life." She sighed and shook her head. "And there are so many other people depending on you."

"What other people?"

"Mr. Williams, for one. He thinks you're coming to the audition. The poor man is dying to make you a star. And then there's David. He's counting on you for the dance. He's already bought the tickets and everything. If you back out on him now—"

"Shut up, Carrie!"

"I'm just trying to help."

"Well, you're doing a lousy job."

Chapter

eight

I hardly slept at all. The next morning, my body ached in places I didn't even know I had. I dragged myself through the house and out the door just in time to miss the bus.

The rest of the day went downhill from there. First, my locker jammed and I had to track down the janitor to jimmy it open. Then we had a pop quiz in science. Then our social studies teacher decided that a 500-word essay on "My Favorite President" was a nice assignment for Monday.

Another weekend down the drain—and I don't even have a favorite president.

In between all that, I had to listen to Lisa bad-mouthing Marsha, while I tried my best to avoid David. I hadn't talked to him since our blow-up the day before, and I still didn't know what I was going to do about the dance.

By the time the final bell rang, I was ready

to resign from the human race.

I had been hoping all day that David would have baseball practice after school. But there he was, standing at my locker, all bright-eyed and bushy-tailed—Mr. Sunshine himself.

"I'm going to take the bus," I said before he could get a word out.

The smile dropped from his face. "Fine, go ahead."

"Don't take it personally, Murdock. I'm just too tired to walk."

"Yeah, I guess covering for Carrie is a pretty tiring job."

I shot him my dirtiest look, but he shot one right back and said, "You're wasting your time, Amy. Carrie's going to get caught, and when she does—"

"Shut up!" I yelled, slamming my locker door so hard I was afraid I'd jammed it again. "This doesn't have anything to do with Carrie, so leave her out of it." I pushed past him and hurried down the hall.

Why was he doing this to me? Why was he so gung-ho on ruining my life?

◆ ◆ ◆ ◆

When I got home, I ran upstairs, stomping my feet until my knees vibrated. Carrie poked her head into the hall. "Don't talk to me," I said as soon as I saw her. But it didn't do any good.

"My, my, aren't we in a good mood."

I ignored her and dashed into my room.

"What's wrong?" she asked, propping herself in my doorway. "Did you have a rough day in kiddie-land?"

I grabbed a book from my desk and threw it at her. But my aim was lousy and it smashed against the wall. She jumped. "What's wrong with you?" she screamed.

"Everything," I screamed back then collapsed on my bed. "Just go away and leave me alone."

She didn't listen. She never listened. I would've had better luck talking to the wall. "Are you still worried about this dance and the play stuff?" she asked.

I pulled the pillow over my head and squished it against my ears.

"Because if you are," she continued, "I have the answer. I know how you can do both."

I tossed the pillow aside and looked at her.

"It's really very simple," she said, inching her way into my room. "The audition is at seven o'clock and the dance starts at eight o'clock. You get dressed for the dance and go to the audition first. I figure it'll be over by nine—nine-thirty tops. Then you go to the dance. You miss the first hour or so, but it takes that long for everyone to relax and start having fun anyway. You'll get there right when things are starting to happen."

She shrugged an *it's-so-simple* kind of shrug and looked at me.

"But what about David?" I asked. "I can't expect him to miss part of the dance because of me."

"He won't miss a minute of it. He can go with Lisa, and you can join him later."

"What?!"

"It's the perfect solution, Amy. Lisa will get to go to the dance with somebody. David won't miss a thing. And you'll get to the audition without missing the best part of the dance. Everyone will come out a winner. Am I brilliant or what?"

I hated to admit it, but it made sense. Still, there was something about it that bothered me. "Lisa will never go along with it," I said.

"She will if you ask her to do it as a favor— and you sound desperate enough. Tell her this audition is the most important thing in your life, but you *can't* let David down. Tell her you're stuck and you *really* need her help. Lay it on thick."

"I don't know, Carrie."

"What's wrong? Are you afraid she'll steal David from you?"

"No! I told you, David and I are just friends."

"Then what's the problem?"

I couldn't explain it. But there was something about David being at that dance with someone else that made me ache inside—and Carrie knew it. I could see it in her eyes. She was standing there, ready to gloat, ready to point her finger and laugh and accuse me of being jealous.

No way! My relationship with David was too fragile for her to stomp on. And I really did want to be in that play. And besides, I couldn't think of another solution.

"There's no problem," I told Carrie. "I'll call Lisa tonight."

But Lisa wasn't the only one I had to convince. I had to talk David into going along with the plan, too. It was one phone call I dreaded making. We'd been arguing so much lately, I wasn't sure how he was going to react.

After supper, Mom and Dad went to the store to pick up the wallpaper they had ordered. As soon as they left, Carrie grabbed her jacket and headed for the back door. "I'll be home in half an hour," she said, tossing the words over her shoulder.

When she was gone, I called David. I told

him about my phone call from Mr. Williams and how the audition was on the same night as the dance and about the plan I had to make it all work out. I told him everything except that the plan was Carrie's idea. Mentioning her name would have been a major disaster.

He listened to the whole story. When I was finished, he said it sounded like a great idea, and he was glad Lisa would get to go to the dance. He also said he knew I'd knock 'em dead at the audition.

He made me feel like I was doing the right thing, like I had nothing to worry about. When we hung up, I felt a hundred pounds lighter.

When I called Lisa next, she wasn't as easy to convince. She had a jillion reasons why it wouldn't work—none of which made any sense.

"You *have* to help me, Lis," I pleaded, taking Carrie's advice about laying it on thick. "I'm desperate! And besides, it's your fault I'm in this mess."

"My fault!"

"Well, partly. You're the one who talked me into going to the audition for the school play. Remember? I didn't want anything to do with it, but you *begged* me to go with you."

"Amy, you landed one of the best parts!"

"Yeah, but Mr. Williams wouldn't know I existed if you hadn't gotten me to go. And that means he wouldn't have called me for this play. So I wouldn't have this problem if I hadn't done *you* a favor."

"All right already. I get the point."

"You mean, you'll do it?"

"Yeah, but only if it's okay with David."

"It is."

All right!

Carrie came flying in the back door just as my parents pulled in the driveway. I couldn't figure out if she planned things that well or if she was just lucky.

"It's all set," I told her. "David and Lisa will go to the dance, and I'll join them after the audition."

We helped Mom and Dad lug everything inside. It took a couple of trips to the car until we were finished. I never saw so much junk. There were dozens of rolls of wallpaper, and cans of something Dad called primer and a lot of funny-looking tools, and a long, narrow plastic thing that looked like a horse trough.

Dad wanted to cart everything into the basement, but Mom wouldn't let him.

"We can't leave all this stuff here," he argued. "It takes up too much room. We'll be tripping over it."

"Exactly," Mom said. "And the more we trip over it, the faster we'll have it hung."

Having half a wallpaper store sitting on our living room floor was going to do wonders for our decor. They finally agreed to store most of it behind the sofa. Dad piled rolls of paper into Carrie's arms so he could maneuver the furniture.

"Oh, Amy," Mom said, "I almost forgot. Mr. Williams pulled up just as we were leaving and he asked me to give you this." She handed me the script for the play. "I was going to tell him about the dance, but I didn't know what you were going to do. Have you decided yet?"

"Yep," I answered. "I'm going to do both. I'll go to the audition first and the dance afterward. I'll miss the first part of the dance. But Carrie said it takes an hour for everyone to loosen up anyway, so I probably won't miss much."

"Are you sure David won't mind being that late?" Mom asked.

"He won't be late," I said, flipping through the script. "He's going to go with—"

There was a loud crash and Mom and I both jumped. Carrie was on the floor. The rolls of wallpaper she had been holding were scattered all over the room.

"Are you all right?" Mom asked, rushing over to help her get up.

"I'm fine. I just tripped over that stupid can," she said.

"I told you this wouldn't work," Dad snapped at Mom. "You can't keep all this stuff in the living room."

"I didn't intend to keep it in the middle of the floor," she snapped back.

They argued while my stomach twisted into a big knot. Carrie bounced up, grabbed my arm, and dragged me to the other side of the room.

"You're such a klutz," I whispered, shaking out of her grip. "You've got them arguing again."

"I did it on purpose, you idiot," she hissed back. "You can't tell Mom that David's going to the dance with Lisa. Mom'll tell you to give the dress back. Then what will you do?"

My heart sank as her words hit me. I almost blew the whole thing. I was never going to be able to pull this off. Never. One little slip, and it would be good-bye dress . . . good-bye dance. Good-bye life.

Chapter
nine

DAVID and Lisa were more excited about the play than I was. They talked about it constantly. By the time the final bell rang on Friday, kids I didn't even know were congratulating me and asking where they could get tickets.

I felt like a star!

Later that night, after Mom and Dad had gone to bed, Carrie and I sat down with a bowl of popcorn and a couple of sodas to watch the video of *West Side Story* that Dad had rented.

"You're going to love this," Carrie said, flicking off the light. "It's a 1950s version of *Romeo and Juliet*."

Great, I thought as the story unfolded. Romeo and Juliet *in the Fifties. I'm not sure this is going to be my kind of movie.*

I slouched in my seat, then shot straight up.

"They're singing and dancing!" I screeched.

"Well, sure," Carrie said. "What did you expect? It's a musical."

"A musical! Mr. Williams said it was about street gangs."

"It is."

"Since when do street gangs sing and dance? I can't sing or dance, Carrie!"

"Will you cool it? The part you're auditioning for is small. You won't have to sing a note."

I settled down and waited for my character to appear. When she did, I almost missed her. That's because *she* looked like a *he*—a street-smart tomboy who was trying to join one of the gangs. Carrie was right. It was a small part, but she popped up at some crucial moments. I liked her spunk—and best of all— she didn't sing or dance!

The movie started out a little slow, but it turned into a real tear-jerker at the end. Carrie and I went through half a box of tissues and I was still sniffling when I climbed into bed. I watched it three more times over the weekend. And if I hadn't had to write that dumb essay on my favorite president, I would have watched it some more.

The week flew by and everything was falling into place. Lisa was so happy she was going to the dance, she started talking to

Marsha again. Then Marsha confessed that she'd had a crush on Denny Houser ever since she met him. And Helen's cousin had a friend who was more than happy to take Patty to the dance.

Best of all, when Mr. Williams called to remind me about the audition (like it was something I could really forget!) and I told him about the dance, he offered to drive me right over to school when my audition was over.

I studied my lines until they were burned into my brain. When Friday rolled around, I felt ready to conquer the world. All I had to do was slip into the dress and get out the door without saying something stupid to Mom (and without breaking my neck on the high heels I was wearing).

I rubbed the silvery knots of my friendship bracelet and went downstairs. My parents ooh'd and ahh'd as soon as they saw me. But Carrie just stood there with a silly smirk on her face.

Dad drove me to the community center and gave me a kiss on the cheek for luck. I kissed him back, grabbed my script, and got out of the car.

◆ ◆ ◆ ◆

"What do you mean, I didn't get the part? I can't believe it! I knew all my lines. I didn't miss a word."

The audition was over and Mr. Williams had pulled me aside to tell me that he was giving my part to someone else.

"I'm sorry, Amy, but this wasn't only my decision. There are several other people who are making the decisions. We all feel that Vanessa would be better for the role."

Vanessa! Vanessa was a fifteen-year-old, bleached blonde who couldn't act her way out of a paper bag. But I had to hand it to her, she came dressed for the part. She wore jeans and sneakers and was able to run around the stage. I practically stood in one spot because of my dress and shoes.

"But you said I was remarkable," I argued. " 'Simply remarkable'—those were your exact words."

"You *were* remarkable in the school play. You *do* have a lot of talent, Amy, but you just didn't look and feel right for the part. Maybe if you'd dressed more appropriately—"

"I told you about the dance!"

"I know," he said. "But I didn't realize it would keep you from acting out the part. Reciting lines wasn't enough for this, Amy. Body language had a lot to do with it—and you just weren't convincing. I'm sorry."

I tried not to cry and I knew Mr. Williams was trying to explain it the best way he could. But it hurt so much. What would I tell all the kids at school? They thought I was a star already. If only I had moved around. If only I hadn't been afraid of turning my ankle or wrinkling my dress or mussing my hair.

If only I could do it all over again.

"Let me try again," I said, wiping the wetness from my eyes. "I can come back tomorrow and I'll run around that stage and you'll see how good I am. You'll see—"

"I'm sorry, Amy. Vanessa has the part. But I'd still like you to be in the play. We can use you as an extra, and, since you know the lines, you'll make the perfect understudy for Vanessa."

An extra and an understudy? That's it? That's what my talent had boiled down to? I was just going to be another body taking up space?

"I don't think so, Mr. Williams."

"I know you're disappointed, Amy. But you'll get some more experience, and the more experience you have—"

"I have better things to do."

I knew I sounded like a sore loser. But I couldn't help it. If I couldn't have a speaking part, why should I waste my time just standing up there?

But Mr. Williams didn't give up. He talked about my "potential" and how I should take advantage of every opportunity I get. He talked as we went out the door and got in his car and drove to school. In fact, he talked so much, I told him I'd think about it just so he'd stop talking.

It wasn't easy walking into the dance all alone. And it wasn't easy facing David and Lisa, who were dying to celebrate my new-found stardom.

It wasn't easy telling them the truth.

I guess they could see how much I was hurting because they said everything they could think of to make me feel better. They said that Mr. Williams was blind, that he didn't know real talent when he saw it, and that I was too good to be in his stupid play anyway.

I wanted to believe them. I stood beneath the balloons and streamers and crepe-paper stars, and I wanted it all to be true.

But I knew it wasn't Mr. Williams's fault. It was mine.

I had blown my one and only chance.

I didn't want to give up anything, and I ended up losing everything. I couldn't even enjoy the dance.

David went to the refreshment table and brought back a plate of food and some punch, but there was a lump in my throat and I knew if I tried to swallow anything, I'd choke.

"Cheer up," Lisa said. "It's not the end of the world. There'll be other plays."

"Not for me," I muttered. The more I thought about my audition, the sicker I felt. I had just stood on the stage, reciting my lines, wanting to get it over with so I could get to the dance. It never occurred to me that someone else could snatch the part away from me. I kept reliving it again and again until I realized how lucky I was that no one had laughed in my face.

And that wasn't even the worst part. The worst part was that I knew if I had tried, I would have done a better job than Vanessa.

For some reason, David and Lisa stuck by my side all night. I knew I was lousy company. I couldn't even tell you what anyone was wearing or who was with whom or what kind of music was playing. I was too angry with myself to notice.

Lisa got a ride home with Marsha and Denny. ("You can't have Mom or Dad taking Lisa home when you told them she wasn't going to be there," Carrie had warned me.)

But Lisa said she didn't mind. She said she was just glad she was able to go to the dance.

When Dad picked David and me up, he was unusually quiet. I had expected him to at least ask how the audition went, but he didn't say a word. After we dropped David off, Dad gave me a funny look and shook his head.

"What's wrong" I asked, but he didn't answer. I figured he had had another fight with Mom and he was still too mad to talk.

When we got home, I wanted to run upstairs and lick my wounds, but Mom was waiting for me when I came in. Carrie was sitting in the recliner, picking nail polish off her thumb, looking positively bored with whatever was going on.

"I was at the mall tonight, Amy," Mom said, standing in front of me. "And I ran into Lisa's mother."

Uh-oh.

"You didn't borrow that dress from Lisa," Mom continued. "Her mother didn't know anything about it. She said Lisa went to the dance with David. Where did you get that dress, Amy?"

I looked at Dad. He was standing at the window, staring into the darkness, his hands jammed in his pockets. Carrie started working on her other thumb.

"Answer me, Amy!" Mom demanded. "Where did you get that dress?"

"F-from Carrie."

"Thanks a lot, Amy," my sister muttered.

"I knew it!" Mom said, spinning toward Carrie. "I *knew* you had something to do with this."

"So what?" Carrie said, jumping to her feet. "So I lent her a dress that you were too cheap to buy. Big deal!"

"And just where did you get it?"

"I borrowed it from someone."

"Who?" Mom asked.

"I don't remember," Carrie said, looking down at her thumb. "It's been hanging in my closet for months."

"You're lying, Carrie," answered Mom. "When you ran away, I tore your room apart looking for some kind of clue that would tell me where you were. I went through every drawer and took everything out of your closet. That dress was not there!"

"Maybe you just don't remember seeing it," Dad said, turning toward us. "You were upset, Elizabeth."

"I *know* I was upset," she snapped. "But that dress *isn't* something I'd forget." Then she looked at Carrie and said, "I want to know where you got that dress, and I want the truth."

Carrie didn't answer.

Time ticked by and I waited along with Mom and Dad. I wanted to hear the truth, too. I wanted to believe she hadn't lied to me, too.

"You aren't going to tell me, are you, Carrie?" Mom asked.

Carrie folded her arms and stared back at Mom so hard that it made me shiver.

"All right, then, you're grounded!" Mom yelled. "And you'll *stay* grounded until you tell me where that dress came from!"

Carrie headed for the stairs.

"And as for you, young lady," Mom said to me, "you're grounded for two weeks."

"What did I do?"

"You lied to me, Amy." She blinked and the tears ran down her cheeks. "I thought I could trust you. You were the one person I thought I could always count on."

My heart twisted and my cheeks were as wet as Mom's. "I-I just wanted to wear a dress from Lucilla's, Mom. That's all," I sobbed through my tears. "I just wanted to wear a dress like this once. Just once."

"Well, I hope it was worth it."

◆ ◆ ◆ ◆

Later, as I sat sniffling on the floor, propped against the side of my bed, I heard Mom and Dad fighting. I couldn't hear their exact words. They were lost in the angry sounds and voices that crashed through the house.

When Carrie came home, I thought everything would be perfect. I thought we'd be a family again. The four of us together under one roof, loving and laughing—that's the way it used to be.

But that hadn't happened.

And somewhere deep inside, I knew it would never be that way again.

What's happened to all of us? I wondered, my thoughts blending into the darkness. *Where has all the laughter gone?*

Chapter

ten

LISA called first thing Saturday morning. Her mom had talked to her about the dress when she got home from the dance, and she was ready to compare notes. But my mom had given me the five-minute signal as soon as I picked up the phone. It was part of the grounding rules in our house. The "groundee" was allowed five minutes per call, which gave you just enough time to explain why you couldn't talk.

Lisa knew the rules as well as I did. So when I told her I was grounded, she sighed and said, "Okay, I'll talk to you on Monday," and hung up.

A little while later David called.

"I'm grounded," I said as soon as I heard his voice. He knew the rules, too. But he still didn't know anything about the dress and I wasn't in the mood to explain it to him. "And it's a long story," I continued, "so don't even ask."

"Why do you put up with her?"

"Who?" I asked, as if I didn't know.

"That idiot sister of yours, that's who."

"What makes you think Carrie had anything to do with this?"

"Because every time you're grounded, she's behind it in one way or another. Why do you put up with it, Amy? Why are you always defending her?"

What was I supposed to say? How do you tell someone that you're trying to hold on to pieces of your life? How do you explain that "putting up" with someone isn't as bad as losing her forever?

You can't, because no one would understand. And that's what I told him. "You don't understand. You don't know what it's like."

"You haven't told your parents about Nick, have you?"

I didn't answer.

"You're making a big mistake, Amy."

I hung up.

I didn't know what hurt the most: my ongoing fight with David or the lies from Carrie . . . blowing the audition or not having anyone even ask me about it . . . bombing out at the dance or the hurt in Mom's eyes when she found out about the dress.

And to make matters even worse, everyone in my family was busy ignoring everyone else. It wasn't until late that afternoon that Mom finally spoke to me.

"Your father and I have to go to a retirement dinner tonight," she said. "It's at the Huntington Lodge. I'll leave the number by the phone."

Her voice was so mechanical, so cold, I half-expected her to say, "This is a recording," at the end. "And don't forget," she added, "you and Carrie are grounded. Don't leave the house."

After they left, I went into the kitchen and Carrie joined me. "So," she said, leaning over the refrigerator door while I rummaged through the leftovers, "how did the audition go?"

I didn't know whether to laugh or cry. It only took twenty-four hours for someone to remember.

"Terrible," I said, suddenly not feeling hungry anymore. I shut the refrigerator door and leaned against the counter. "I didn't get the part. Some bubble-brain named Vanessa got it."

"What happened? I thought Mr. Williams was ready to put your name in lights."

I told her the whole story. When I was finished, she just stood there with a silly smirk on her face. I had seen that smirk before. Last night! When I was leaving for the audition!

"You knew!" I started to cry as the truth hit me. I guess I was too excited about the movie to notice what Carrie had noticed. "You set me up!"

"What?"

"You knew the part I was auditioning for, Carrie. You knew I couldn't act it out dressed the way I was. That's why you looked at me that way last night! That's why you're looking at me that way now! You knew I was going to blow it—and you've been dying for me to tell you!"

I wanted her to deny it. I wanted her to tell me that I was crazy, that I didn't know what I was talking about. That she'd never do something like that to me.

I wanted her to say something—anything— that would take away the pain.

But she didn't. She just stood there, trying to wipe the smirk off her face, but it wouldn't budge.

"Why, Carrie? Why didn't you warn me?" The tears flooded my eyes. "Why do you hate me so much?"

She spun around and walked away, but I

followed her. "Why?" I repeated through the dining room and living room and into the hall, where she grabbed her jacket and headed for the door.

"Where are you going?" I screamed.

"Out," she snapped.

"You can't go anywhere! You're grounded!"

"Who's going to stop me?"

The door slammed and she was gone. I was left there, wondering if she was ever coming back, wondering if I even wanted her to.

I ran upstairs and threw myself on the bed, screaming and crying and pounding my pillow until I couldn't cry anymore.

Why, Carrie, why? I shut my eyes, wishing more than anything that I could shut out the world and create another one in its place.

I must've fallen asleep because the next thing I knew, it was ten-thirty and my mouth felt like a wad of cotton. I went into the bathroom, splashed some water on my face, and rinsed out my mouth. Then I went downstairs to get something to drink.

Carrie was half-sitting, half-lying on the sofa, looking like someone had just dumped her there. "Well, well," she said, grabbing a long-necked bottle from the table beside her, "look who's here. It's my little shishter."

Huh? Her little what?

"What's wrong, Amsy?"

Amsy?

"You shtill ticked off at me?"

All my crying must have made my brain soggy, because her words sounded like mush. I stepped closer as she took a swig from the bottle. The label glared at me. It was vodka! "You're drunk! I don't believe this. Are you crazy? Where did you get that stuff?"

"Oh, loosen up, will ya? It's party time."

"You got that bottle from Nick, didn't you?"

"Now don't you go saying anything bad 'bout my friend Nicky." She tried to shake her finger at me, but she couldn't quite get the hang of it.

"You're crazy! When Mom and Dad find out that you've been drinking—"

"They're not gonna find out 'cause you're not gonna tell them . . . are you?"

I wanted to. I wanted to pick up the phone right then and there and call them and tell them that their daughter was smashed and that I wasn't going to put up with it anymore. But I couldn't do it.

I couldn't stand the thought of another fight.

I didn't want to see the hurt in Mom's eyes, or hear the anger in Dad's voice, or listen to the accusations they'd fling at each other.

Just thinking about how it would be made

me want to cry.

"Ahhh, what's wrong, Amy? You look so shad. Don't you want to party with me?"

"No!"

I turned and headed for the kitchen. Carrie followed—or at least she tried to. I could hear her stumbling around behind me, but I refused to turn around and look.

"The room's spinning," she said as I searched for a can of soda in the fridge. "Amy, I don't feel so hot."

"Gee, I wonder why."

"I mean it . . . Amy. I—"

The crash made me jump and when I looked behind me, Carrie was sprawled on the floor. Her eyes were closed and there was blood trickling from the side of her head. The vodka bottle was shattered around her.

"Carrie!" I screamed. I fell on my knees beside her and tried to shake her awake. But she just lay there like a broken doll.

I'd seen dead people before, but they were old people in caskets, surrounded by flowers.

I didn't know what young dead people looked like.

I didn't know if Carrie was still alive.

"Carrieee!" I screamed so loud, my head throbbed from the strain. But she didn't move. Her eyelids didn't even flutter.

I pushed myself up and ran to the phone. 9-1-1. *Three simple numbers,* I told myself. *You can dial three simple numbers.* But it seemed to take forever, and it took even longer for someone to answer.

I told the voice on the other end that I needed an ambulance. I told it to hurry. I told it my name and address and that Carrie was lying on the floor with blood coming out of her head and that I couldn't wake her up.

"Is she breathing?" the voice asked me.

"Will you *please* send an ambulance!" I yelled.

"Calm down. There's an ambulance on the way. Is your sister breathing?"

"I don't know. I can't tell."

"Put your ear next to her nose and tell me if you feel anything, but don't hang up."

The voice didn't have to worry. I wasn't about to lose my only connection with sanity. With our extra-long cord, I was able to hold on to the phone and bend over Carrie's face at the same time. A warm stream of air tickled my ear, and I cried with relief, "She's breathing. I can feel it."

"Good girl. Now, do you know how to find a pulse?"

"No . . . yeah. I don't know. I can't think!"

"Do you know where the Adam's apple is?"

"Yeah, it's in the throat."

"Right. Put your fingers in the hollow spot next to her Adam's apple and tell me if you feel anything there."

As soon as I found the hollow spot in her throat, it all came back to me. "I know how to do this," I told the voice. "We do it in gym class all the time." What was wrong with me? Why did it take so long for that memory to pop into place?

And why didn't I feel anything in Carrie's neck?

"It's not there!" I screamed. "I don't feel anything!"

"Push in a little deeper and keep your fingers absolutely still. Her pulse won't be pounding like yours does in gym class."

I pushed a little deeper, but my hands were shaking and I had to hold my breath to keep them still. Then I felt it. The voice was right. Carrie's pulse wasn't pounding. It was more like a quiver, and I could hardly feel it. But it was definitely there.

"I found it. But it's not very strong."

The voice didn't answer.

"Hello, hello. Are you still there? Don't leave me now!"

"I'm here, Amy. We've got an ETA of five minutes. Estimated time of arrival. The ambulance should be there in five minutes."

Five minutes. That wasn't very long, was it? I mean, people didn't die in five minutes, did they?

I knelt beside Carrie, clutching the phone, staring at her face, wanting her to wake up and tell me that this whole thing was just a joke. One big, huge joke.

I stared at her mouth, wanting to see that stupid smirk of hers one more time.

Come on, Carrie. I won't get mad, I promise. Say it's all a big joke.

I just stared, hoping and praying. And then I saw something that hadn't been there before.

"Oh, no!" I screamed into the phone.

"What's wrong?"

"Her lips are turning blue!"

"Calm down, Amy."

"Tell them to hurry! Please, tell them to hurry!"

Chapter
eleven

IT looked as if the paramedics had brought half the hospital with them. There was a small oxygen tank and a mask (which they slapped on Carrie's face the second they saw her), a stethoscope and blood pressure cuff, and a whole suitcase full of medicine, needles, and miles of plastic tubing.

"How much of this stuff did she drink?" the taller paramedic asked as he pushed chunks of the broken vodka bottle aside with his foot. He had pitch-black hair and a mustache that looked like it was still growing in.

"I don't know." I was trying to see if Carrie's lips were still blue. But the oxygen mask covered her nose and mouth, and I couldn't tell. "A lot, I think."

"Where are your parents?" the other one asked. He had blond hair and blue eyes and muscles that Arnold Schwarzenegger would envy.

"They are at a retirement party at the Huntington Lodge. They left the number." I pulled it off the phone and handed it to him. He handed it to the man with the mustache, who stuffed it in his shirt pocket.

"Her head is bleeding," I told them.

The muscular one glanced at the puddle of blood while he wrapped a blood pressure cuff around Carrie's arm. "Did she take any drugs?" he asked.

"No."

It was an automatic response and I knew as soon as I said it I had to change it. A couple of hours ago, I would've said that she didn't drink either. "I mean, I don't know. I'm not sure. She didn't say anything about drugs and I didn't see any. Is she going to be okay?"

"How about prescription drugs?" he asked as he pulled her eyelids back and flashed a light into her eyes. "Diet pills, sleeping pills, Valium—anything like that?"

"N-no, I don't think so."

He ripped the velcro cuff off her arm and asked, "Any medical problems? Diabetes, heart disease . . .?"

"No." It was the only thing I was sure of. "Is she going to be okay?"

They still didn't answer. They were too busy tossing words and numbers back and

102

forth. When they were finished, they lifted Carrie onto a stretcher and wheeled her out of the house.

The man with the mustache jumped in the driver's seat while the other man and I stayed in the back of the ambulance with Carrie. I sat right across from her head in case she woke up. I wanted her to see me as soon as she opened her eyes. I didn't want her to be afraid.

I heard the guy with the mustache talking into some kind of radio. He was telling someone about Carrie. He was telling them that she was fifteen and unconscious, and that she had a head laceration. He said that she had been drinking and that there was no evidence of drugs. Then he rattled off all the numbers that he and the other man had rattled off in the kitchen.

Then he pulled a paper out of his shirt pocket and told them my parents' phone number. "It's the Huntington Lodge," he said. "Our ETA—fifteen minutes."

We flew through the streets. The paramedic kept one hand on Carrie's pulse and both eyes on her face. There was a clear bag hanging at the end of her oxygen mask. You could tell she was breathing by the way the bag emptied and filled.

We turned a corner and Carrie made a funny noise. The paramedic pushed me out of the way, tore off the oxygen mask, and loosened her safety belt. He turned her until her head was hanging over the side. Then he grabbed a kidney-shaped bowl and stuck it under her mouth just in time for her to throw up.

The whole ambulance smelled like rot. I almost gagged.

When she was finished, he moved her back into place, wiped her mouth, and slipped the mask back on. Carrie didn't even wake up. She had just barfed her guts out, and she didn't even know it!

We turned another corner and Carrie's head rolled with the movement. Her face turned chalky white.

"She's going to be okay, isn't she?" I asked. "I mean, people don't die from drinking, do they?"

"That depends," the paramedic said.

"On what?" I asked.

"On how much they had to drink."

◆ ◆ ◆ ◆

They wouldn't let me stay with Carrie at the hospital. I begged and pleaded, but they just asked me a lot of questions. Then a nurse with copper-colored hair whisked me down the hall.

"You can wait in there," she said, pointing to a doorway. "We've notified your parents and they're on their way." She was gone before I could argue.

You could tell it was a waiting room by the molded plastic orange seats and the fake plants and the piles of magazines stacked on a table. Except for an old man sitting in the corner, the room was empty.

I parked myself in one of the orange buckets and gripped the sides so I wouldn't slide off. The old man didn't look at me. He was too busy playing with his hat. Around and around it went, the brim sliding through his fingers over and over and over again. I kept my mind off Carrie by counting the revolutions. I was up to ten when a doctor walked in. He was wearing baggy green pants and a matching green top and his white shoes were speckled with blood. He didn't look at me either. He walked over to the old man.

"Mr. Daubert," he said.

The hat stopped. The old man straightened in his seat.

"I'm sorry, sir," the doctor said. "There was nothing we could do."

"You mean, Martha's dead?"

"I'm sorry, sir."

My eyes were glued to the old man. It was like watching a movie unfold on the screen. Except then he looked right at me and my heart stood still. "She's gone," he said in a hoarse voice, his eyes filling with tears. "My Martha's gone. We've been together fifty-four years. Married fifty-four years—and now she's up and left me."

The nurse with copper hair came out of nowhere and helped the old man to his feet. "Fifty-four years," he told her, releasing me from his gaze. "How could she leave me after fifty-four years?"

The nurse didn't answer. She just patted his back in a *there, there* kind of way. She and the doctor ushered him out of the room. Outside, the P.A. system was going crazy. It was paging doctors left and right, while static filled the spots in between.

I tightened my grip on the seat and stared at a mangled copy of *Time* that someone had tossed on the floor. I kept trying to get the old man out of my mind, but he wouldn't budge.

Is that what was going to happen to me? Was some guy in green pajamas going to come in and tell me that he was sorry . . . that there was nothing he could do . . . that Carrie was gone and she was never coming back?

Is that what happened in these plastic-coated rooms? I sucked in some air and held it as long as I could. That's when I heard my parents coming. Mom's high heels were clicking against the floor like a tap dance version of morse code. Click . . . click, click . . . click, click . . . click. I jumped up and rushed to the door. They came in just as I got there. Mom grabbed my shoulders. "Amy, what happened? Where's Carrie?"

I didn't want to answer any more questions. I wanted them to take me home, tuck me in bed, and tell me everything was okay.

"Amy!" Mom shook me, knocking the dream out of my head. "What happened to Carrie?"

"She was drinking and she p-passed out and—"

"Drinking!" Dad snapped. "You called an *ambulance* because she had too much to drink?"

"But I couldn't wake her up! And she hit her head and there was blood all over the place and—"

"You should have called *us!*" he said. "We left the number taped to the phone. Couldn't you dial it?"

"Peter," Mom said in a squirmy voice. "Not so loud."

"I don't care! I don't believe this! We leave two teenage girls alone in the house for a couple of hours, and look where we are! What do we have to do? Hire a baby-sitter every time we want to go out?"

"That's not fair," I said, choking on a fresh batch of tears. "You weren't there. You didn't see her. You don't know—"

"I'm going to look for a doctor," he told Mom. But he didn't have to go very far. Another guy in green was coming up the hall with a clipboard in his hand. He headed straight for them. "Mr. and Mrs. Phillips?"

They nodded.

"I'm Dr. Salazar."

"How's Carrie?" Mom asked.

I held my breath. *Please, let her be all right!*

"She seems to be doing fine right now, but we'd like to keep her here for a few days."

"Keep her?" Dad was still fuming. "You just said she was fine!"

"I said she seems to be doing fine right now. She has ten stitches in her head and a severe concussion. Add that to a bottle of vodka and you've got a dangerous combination. She's not out of the woods yet."

"Vodka?" Mom asked, then looked at Dad. "We don't have any vodka in the house, do we?"

"No. We've got some wine, and there may

be a little brandy left. But there's no vodka."

"Then where did she get it?" asked Mom.

"From Nick," I said and all three heads swiveled in my direction.

"What?!?!" Mom said. "You can't mean Nick Rafferty!"

I nodded and waited for Dad's reaction, but he didn't have one. "Carrie's been hanging around with him for a couple of weeks," I added.

It was a good thing we were in a hospital because Mom looked like she was going to faint. "Why didn't you tell me," she asked. "Why didn't you say something?"

"I couldn't!" I shouted. "Carrie said if I told you, she'd run away again, and she'd never come back." Just repeating her words sent a chill down my spine. "What was I supposed to do, Mom? Huh? What was I *supposed* to do?"

We were both crying.

"Will you two please calm down?" Dad said. "We can discuss this at home."

Dr. Salazar stepped closer to Mom and said, "We have a very good social service department here. If you're having a problem with Carrie, and you'd like to talk to them about family counseling, I can arrange—"

"We don't have a problem," Dad snapped. "And we don't need a counselor. We have a rebellious teenage daughter who had too much to drink."

"And you don't consider that a problem?" the doctor asked.

"No!" Dad snapped again. "All kids drink. It's a phase they go through. Why are you making such a big thing out of it? It isn't like she was on drugs."

"Alcohol *is* a drug, Mr. Phillips. And when a fifteen-year-old girl picks up a bottle, she has a problem. Now you can ignore it or deny it or call it a phase. But the fact is, your daughter was brought in here unconscious. There was someone to help her this time. The next time, she may not be so lucky."

Dad went white. He looked as if someone had pulled a plug and all the blood had drained out of him.

"Who do we call?" Mom asked. "How do we get help?"

"Elizabeth, please," Dad muttered. "We'll talk about it later."

"No, we won't," she said. "There's nothing to talk about. I'm going to see a counselor, and I'm taking Carrie with me. And you can do whatever you darn well please."

"Elizabeth—"

"I want to hold our marriage together, Peter. But I'm not going to sacrifice my children for it."

They wouldn't let me see Carrie. Mom and Dad got to see her, Dr. Salazar made sure of that, but not me. I was shuffled back into the waiting room—put away until someone needed me again.

People drifted in and out of the room, but no one sat in the corner seat. It was as if the old man was still sitting there and no one wanted to disturb him.

I wondered what happened to him. How was he going to live without Martha?

What does it feel like to be all alone?

What do you do when your family's gone?

◆ ◆ ◆ ◆

"Don't worry, honey," Mom said as we got in the car. "Carrie will be okay."

"Is she awake?"

"Sort of."

Sort of? "Is she or isn't she?"

"Well," Mom said, fumbling with the strap of her purse, "she's . . . she's . . ."

"She's drunk," Dad finished for her.

"She'll be fine tomorrow," Mom added. "She just has to sleep it off."

"And she could have done that at home," Dad said.

"Peter, you heard the doctor!"

"He was just trying to scare us, Elizabeth. That's how these doctors operate. If you hadn't fallen apart, he never would have said the things he did. And if Amy had called us instead of the paramedics, Carrie would be sleeping in her own bed tonight."

Mom didn't answer. I just sat in the backseat, staring at the dark space between them, wishing we could've brought Dr. Salazar home with us . . . wishing there was someone who could make Dad understand.

"Her lips were blue," I said quietly.

"What?" Mom swung around to face me and I met Dad's eyes in the rearview mirror.

"She was lying on the floor with her head cracked open and I couldn't wake her up. And then her lips turned blue." I started crying and shaking and gasping for air.

"Amy, it's okay," Mom said, reaching over the seat, trying to touch me. "Carrie will be okay, honey. You'll see. She'll be home before you know it."

"But Martha died!"

"Martha? Who's Martha?" Mom asked.

"I don't know. But she shouldn't have died. She shouldn't have left him all alone."

Chapter

twelve

I didn't see Carrie the next day either. Mom and Dad spent hours at the hospital. They said I could come along, but I decided to wait. According to everything I had heard, Carrie was going to make a full recovery. And I needed some time alone, time to unload my brain and sort things out.

So much had happened so fast.

I had been trying to hold all of us together. I was trying so hard and then—*whammo*—it was over. It was as if someone had picked us all up and thrown us in the air and we had all landed in different spots.

Carrie had been drowning herself in alcohol. Mom and Dad seemed about to get divorced. And I couldn't reach any of them. I couldn't stretch myself that far.

I couldn't pick up the pieces and glue us back together.

Not this time.

We were too far apart.

◆ ◆ ◆ ◆

"Just say it, Murdock, okay? Just spit it out.
Get it over with. Put me out of my misery."

It was Monday afternoon, and David was
walking with me to the hospital. Carrie was
being discharged, and Mom said that if I
wanted to visit with her after school, she'd
pick us both up after work.

I hadn't expected David to tag along. But
once he heard what had happened on Saturday
night, I couldn't get rid of him. Every time I
turned around, he was there—and he didn't say
a thing about what happened. Not one word!
It was driving me crazy!

"Well, what do you want me to say?" he
asked.

"'Told-you-so,'" I said in a sing-song voice.
"Go on, say it. 'I told you Nick was bad news.
I told you to tell your parents. I told you Carrie
was heading for big trouble.' Will you just say
it so I can get on with my life?"

"I don't have to say it. I figure you know all
that by now."

He was right. I did know all that now, and
I knew a lot of other things, too. I knew that

114

having people trust you was more important than what you wore to a dance. I knew that Lisa's friendship meant just as much to me as David's—and friendships were deeper than dates.

And I knew now that I had to stand up to Carrie. We turned a corner and the hospital loomed ahead. It looked different in the daytime. Bathed in sunlight, it seemed like just another building. But inside, nothing had changed. There were people all over the place, and the P.A. system was humming the same old tune.

"Carrie's on the fourth floor," I told him as we plowed through the lobby. "There should be elevators around here somewhere."

"Do you want me to wait for you?"

"Wait? I thought you wanted to see her."

"Are you kidding? She's the last person in the world I want to see," he said.

"Then what are you doing here?"

"I don't know," he said with a shrug.

"You hiked all the way over here and you don't know why?"

He didn't answer. He didn't have to. It was written in his eyes.

"Uh, there's an elevator," he said, pointing behind me. "If you want me to wait, I will."

"No, that's okay." I headed down the hall,

then stopped. "Hey, Murdock!" I shouted. He turned toward me. "Thanks."

"For what?"

For being there, I thought as I rubbed the knots of my bracelet. *For always knowing when I need someone. I like you, Murdock. I really, really like you.*

"I don't know," I said with a shrug.

He shifted his weight from one foot to the other, cocked his head, and smiled.

Mom had told me that Carrie was on the fourth floor. "The adolescent ward," Mom had said. But when I got off the elevator, I thought I landed on *Sesame Street.* There were letters and numbers painted on the walls, and the hall was filled with little kids in baggy pajamas clinging to their mothers' hands.

"Carrie Phillips?" I asked the first nurse I saw.

"Down the hall," she said. "Last door on your right."

Some kid started screaming bloody murder and I high-tailed it to Carrie's room. She didn't seem to mind the commotion. She was sitting on the bed, playing checkers with a mop-haired little boy who told me that his name was Todd and he was six years old.

"You're not six," Carrie said. "You're five."

"But I'll be six someday," he said.

"Yeah, but don't rush it. You're only young once you know."

He laughed as he jumped her last piece. "I win again," he screeched and swept the checkers off the board. Before I knew it, he was gone.

"Cute kid," I said as Carrie closed the checker board and slid it to the end of her bed. "What's he in here for?"

"Some kind of breathing problem. He wheezes a lot."

"Oh." I propped myself on the edge of a windowsill that was big enough to be a seat.

Carrie sank against her pillow and stared straight ahead. Her face was pale and her lips looked like washed out pieces of flesh. A small section of hair was matted with dried blood, and I figured the stitches were somewhere underneath.

I had a lot on my mind, a lot of things I needed to say. But now that I was there, I didn't know where to start It had seemed so easy when I had rehearsed it. I took a deep breath and started talking, just like I had planned to.

"I'm not covering for you anymore, Carrie." The words fell out of my mouth and bounced around the room, but Carrie didn't seem to notice. She just stared straight ahead.

"And I don't care what you say," I continued. "You can make all the threats you want, it won't matter."

Still nothing.

"I should've told Mom about Nick the first time I saw you with him. But I didn't want to lose you again. I thought that was the worst thing that could happen—but it wasn't."

Why don't you say something?

"Seeing you on the floor with blood coming out of your head and watching your lips turn blue—that was the worst thing. And I never want to see it again. So if you want to hang out with people like Nick and drink until you pass out . . . well, then maybe you should just leave. Because I don't want to watch you die."

There, it was—out. I'd said everything I wanted to say. And now I couldn't even look at her. I pushed myself off the windowsill. "Tell Mom I'm walking home," I said and headed for the door.

"I don't hate you, Amy."

I froze.

"And I didn't set you up for that audition. I really thought my plan would work, until we watched the movie. That's when I realized you'd never get the part dressed the way you were. You'd never be able to act it out."

"Why didn't you warn me?"

"Because I was sick and tired of hearing how talented you are." Her voice cracked and she blinked back the tears. "That's all Dad ever talks about, you know. You and that stupid school play you were in."

"W-what are you talking about, Carrie? He hasn't mentioned that in ages."

"Not to *you*, but that's all I ever hear about. And after Mr. Williams called, it got worse. That's when Mom got into the act. The way they talked, you were ready for an Oscar."

I just stared at her.

"So, I decided to keep my mouth shut. I thought if you were as great as they said you were, you didn't need me to warn you. You'd figure it out yourself. And if you didn't . . . well, then Mom and Dad would realize that I wasn't the only one who could screw things up."

I tried to keep my hands from shaking. But I couldn't.

"I didn't do it to hurt you, Amy," she continued. "I did it to prove a point."

"You used me to prove a point?"

"I didn't think the play was that important. I mean, you couldn't decide if you even wanted to audition for it. And then you moaned and groaned because it was a musical. I didn't think it mattered if you got the part. I thought all you really cared about was the dance."

119

Suddenly, I couldn't hold what I was feeling inside anymore.

"How would you know what I cared about?" I screamed at her. "You never think about anyone but yourself!"

A nurse rushed into the room and gave me a dirty look. "You'll have to leave," she said quickly, gesturing toward the door.

She didn't have to say it twice.

Chapter

thirteen

AFTER spilling our guts out in the hospital, Carrie and I didn't have anything to say to each other when she came home.

Mom took a leave of absence from her job. "I just need some time to think," she explained. But she wasn't fooling me. I knew she was afraid to take her eyes off Carrie for a minute.

And Dad—well, Dad did what he always does when there's trouble in the air. He spent almost every waking hour at his office. And when he did come home, he was so busy ignoring Mom, he didn't have time for anything else.

No one was talking to anyone.

Silence filled our house until the walls bulged. And every morning I woke up with the same headache I went to bed with. I felt as if I was waiting for a bomb to go off and I couldn't warn anyone. I was afraid if I opened my mouth, I'd light the fuse.

So when Mom announced that she had called the Family Service Agency and was seeing a therapist, I was relieved. And when she said that she had made an appointment for Carrie too, I was thrilled.

But when she told me that I was next, my eyes bugged out. "Me! Why me?" I sputtered. "I'm not the one with the problem!"

"Honey, we can't go on living like this," she said. "We have to get to the bottom of it. We have to get things straightened out."

"What about Dad?" I snapped at her. "When is he going?"

Her eyes filled with tears. "Amy, please, don't make this any harder than it already is."

"But, Mom—"

"Amy, *please*. Do it for me."

So on a Monday afternoon, two weeks after Carrie had been discharged from the hospital, Mom picked me up after school. She deposited me in another waiting room, where I sat and stared at another pile of magazines.

My hands were clammy and I had a horrible pain in the pit of my stomach. Why did I let her talk me into this? What do you say to a therapist? What if I said the wrong thing? Could I take it back and start all over?

What am I doing here!?!?

A few minutes later, Mrs. Killian appeared. She was thirtyish with short blond hair and the greenest eyes I've ever seen. Mom introduced her as our therapist, then looked at me and said, "I'll pick you up in an hour."

Pick me up? What's she talking about? "I thought you were staying with me! I thought we were doing this together!"

"I'd prefer to see you alone, Amy," Mrs. Killian said before Mom could answer. "But if you're that uncomfortable . . ." She looked at Mom and Mom looked at me. I just stood there feeling like a two-year-old and hating every second of it.

"I'm not uncomfortable," I said. "I just had the wrong idea, that's all."

Mom gave me a quick hug and left. Mrs. Killian took me into a tiny cubicle she called her office. It was crammed with plants and pottery, and there was a goldfish bowl on her desk. I sat down and watched two fish chase each other through a plastic castle while Mrs. Killian sat in a chair behind her desk.

"Do you like fish?" she asked.

"They're okay," I said.

"They're supposed to be very relaxing to watch. I'd love to have an aquarium, but I just don't have the space."

I didn't say anything.

She talked about the weather and asked if I was looking forward to summer vacation. I said exactly what I was supposed to say. "I can't wait," I said, which was a total lie. School was the only place I could go to talk to people who talked back to me. The play would have been the perfect substitute. But now, thanks to Carrie, I didn't even have that.

I noticed the fish had gotten tired of their castle and were now just cruising slowly around the bowl.

"Do you know why you're here, Amy?"

Bingo. There it was, the million-dollar question, and I didn't have an answer. I didn't even how what I was supposed to say. I glanced at my watch. Fifty minutes to go. I had to come up with something.

"Not really," I finally said. It was the safest thing I could think of

"Didn't your mother talk to you?"

"Yeah, kind of."

"What did she say?"

"That we had to get things straightened out. That we can't go on living like this. But—"

"But what?"

"But I don't have the answers! I don't know why Carrie does the things she does!"

124

"That's why you think you're here? To answer for Carrie?"

"Sure. Why else would I be here? She's the one who needs to be straightened out."

Mrs. Killian leaned forward and gave me a gentle smile. "You're not here to supply answers, Amy. You're here because your family is going through a rough time right now. A lot of families hit rough spots along the way. Some of them work it out on their own, others ask for help."

"But I don't need help. Carrie's the one who has a problem. *She's* the one who drank the vodka."

"And you were the only one home when she passed out," she said. "That must have been pretty scary."

It was the first time anyone had said anything about what I had gone through that night. Suddenly I knew I wanted to talk about it. I wanted someone to listen.

"Her lips were blue," I said. "But Dad yelled at me for calling 9-1-1. He said I should have called them instead. He said Carrie was just drunk and she could have slept it off at home."

The tears formed behind my eyes. I looked at her, wanting an answer to a question I was too afraid to ask.

"You did the right thing, Amy," she said.

Tears of relief ran down my face.

"If your father had been there," she continued, "he would have done the same thing. You acted very responsibly."

"Then why did he yell at me?"

"I don't know. I can't speak for your father. But I can tell you that some parents won't admit that their child has a problem. And they get very angry when someone points it out to them. I don't know if that's what happened between you and your dad. Maybe he just didn't realize how serious the situation was. Whatever his reason, he shouldn't have yelled at you."

I could feel tears of relief coming to my eyes.

"You did the right thing, Amy. So don't feel guilty."

She was saying everything I wanted to hear. She was trying so hard to make me feel better—and I didn't deserve it!

"But it was all my fault," I blurted. "I knew Carrie was heading for trouble when I saw her with Nick, but I didn't say anything. I didn't want her to run away again. But then she almost died. I almost killed her." My cheeks were soaked and my nose was running and there wasn't a tissue in sight.

"You're *not* responsible for what Carrie did,"

Mrs. Killian said as she pulled a box of tissues from a shelf and handed them to me. "You're not responsible for anyone's actions but your own."

"But if I had told my parents, Carrie wouldn't have ended up in the hospital," I said, mopping my face with a wad of tissues. "None of this would have happened." *She would've just disappeared instead,* I thought and cried some more.

"You don't know what would have happened, Amy," she said softly. "Yes, you should have told your parents. You were wrong in keeping that information from them. But I can understand the dilemma you were in. It wasn't an easy decision to make. It wasn't an easy decision for *anyone* to make. It's hard being stuck in the middle."

Stuck. That's exactly how I felt.

Stuck between my parents and Carrie.

Stuck holding pieces that wouldn't fit together anymore.

"It was hard," I told her. "It still is."

"*That's* why you're here, Amy. You see, it doesn't matter who has the problem. Carrie's actions have affected everyone. Your mom, your dad—and you. And you've all reacted differently."

I nodded and sniffled at the same time.

"You've all been trying to cope in your own

ways," she continued. "And sometimes when that happens, the family unit falls apart. Everyone's so busy trying to find his or her own answers, the family can't function as a whole. They just can't work together."

"Is that what's happening to us?"

"I think so."

"You mean, we're broken?"

"Sort of."

"Can you fix us?"

"No. But I can point each of you in the right direction so you can fix yourselves. But whether it works depends on how hard each of you is willing to try."

"Do you think we have a chance?"

"Yes. I think you have a very good chance. Admitting there is a problem and asking for help is half the battle."

But what about Dad? I wondered. *He isn't even talking to any of us. Can we fix ourselves without him?* I wanted to ask, but I was afraid I'd lose the thread of hope she was dangling in front of me. I wasn't ready to have it snatched away. Not yet. I wanted to go on believing a little while longer.

We spent the rest of the hour talking about me. Just me. She didn't think I was crazy when I told her that there were times when I didn't know if I loved Carrie or hated her.

She said that being confused was normal, and then she explained that I could love Carrie and still hate the things that she did. She said that one feeling didn't automatically eliminate the other. She said it was all right to be angry and disappointed . . . and scared. And then she stressed how important it was for me to tell my parents if I knew Carrie was doing something that could harm her.

"You don't have to worry about that," I said. "I've already told Carrie I'm not covering for her anymore."

"I'm glad to hear that, Amy. But I have to warn you, it may not be easy. When we care about someone, we don't want to risk losing them. There's always a part of us that thinks if we keep our mouths shut, the problem will go away. But I can tell you, that doesn't happen. Some problems won't go away on their own. If you ignore them, they just get bigger."

I know you're right about that.

"When you cover for someone, you're only helping her to destroy herself. Do you know what I'm saying, Amy? Do you understand?"

"Yeah, I know all that now," I explained. "Every time I think of Carrie lying on that floor, I know I should have told my parents what was going on. But then again I wonder what good it would have done. Carrie would

129

have just disappeared again. Would that have been any better?"

"Do you think your parents would have let that happen?"

"I don't know," I said with a shrug. "I don't know if they could have stopped her. Once Carrie makes up her mind about something, she doesn't let anyone stand in her way—especially my parents."

I paused for a second, then added, "I don't think they know how to handle her. I don't think they know how to help."

"How can they," she asked, "if they don't know what's going on?"

"But sometimes they don't even listen!" I snapped, then bit my tongue.

"Amy. I'm not saying your parents are perfect. Sure, they've made mistakes, and they'll probably make more. We all make mistakes with our children. But Carrie is *their* responsibility. They have to help her and guide her and protect her the best way *they* know how. It's *their* job to raise her—not yours."

"Then what am I supposed to do? Just sit back and keep my fingers crossed?"

"Of course not. There are a lot of things you can do to help."

"Like what?" I asked. I sure couldn't figure it out!

"Well, to start with, you can cooperate with your parents' decision about counseling." She leaned back in her chair and gave me another smile. "Your mother told me you weren't happy about coming here today."

My cheeks got hot.

"It was a very difficult decision for them to make, Amy. They need your support."

They? She made it sound like Mom and Dad were joined at the hip. I didn't have the guts to tell her she was wrong.

There were other things I wanted to talk about, other questions I wanted to ask. But our time was up. And you know what? Even though I didn't want to come to see her in the first place, I didn't want to leave!

"We'll be seeing each other again," she said as if she had read my mind. "In the meantime, I'd like you to think of other ways you can help your family without interfering with your parents' responsibility."

"I thought *you* were going to tell me how to do that."

"I can offer some suggestions, but you know your parents and sister better than I do. You know their strengths and weaknesses. You know where they need your support."

I just shrugged.

"And there's one other person you have

to think about."

"Who?" Huh? Did she think there was someone else in our family?

"Yourself. You can't change what has happened, Amy, but you can learn from it. We all make mistakes, that's part of growing up. And you know what? We'll keep on making mistakes. The best we can hope for is that we don't make the same one twice."

I felt like I'd made enough mistakes already to last me a lifetime.

"Don't punish yourself for being human, Amy. Be good to yourself. Oh, yes—make a list of things you can do to help and bring it with you the next time you come. We'll go over it together."

I nodded and wandered into the waiting room. There was Dad, sitting by the window, reading *Sports Illustrated*.

"I thought Mom was picking me up."

He jumped at the sound of my voice. "She is," he said as he stood, tossing the magazine aside. "She's double-parked outside."

"Then what are you doing here?" I asked.

"Mr. Phillips?" The voice came from behind me. I turned around and Mrs. Killian was standing there. She introduced herself to Dad and they shook hands while I squeezed the soggy clump of tissues in my fist.

"Mom didn't tell me you were coming," I said. "She didn't say a word."

He pulled at his ear and straightened his tie. "I guess she was afraid I'd change my mind."

I squeezed the tissues tighter. "I'm glad you didn't change your mind. I'm glad you're here."

He looked at me, his eyes darting over my face as if he was seeing me for the first time. "Me, too," he said, running his thumb over a wet spot under my eye. "Me, too."

◆ ◆ ◆ ◆

That night after supper, Mom and Dad announced that they were going for a walk. "It's part of our therapy," Mom explained as we all helped to clear the table. "Mrs. Killian wants us to spend half an hour alone together every day. It doesn't matter what we do—"

"As long as we don't fight," Dad interrupted with a wink.

Mom smiled. She had a great smile. It was one of those full-face smiles—you know, when the eyes crinkle and the skin practically glows and the entire room seems to light up from it. I hadn't seen it in such a long time, I'd forgotten how great it really was.

After they left, Carrie and I did the dishes.

The click-clack of plates and silverware, and the sloshy sound of soapy water filled up the empty space between us.

"So," Carrie said when we were almost finished, "what did you think of Mrs. Killian?"

It was the first time she had mentioned a word about counseling. In fact, it was the first time she had said *anything* to me in quite a while. I'd grown so used to our silence that her voice caught me off guard.

"Uh, I liked her," I answered, holding Mom's smile in my head while I tried not to squirm. "How about you?"

"She's okay, I guess. I'd like her better if she hadn't given me a stupid assignment to do. I've been working on it for days."

"What do you have to do?"

"Make a list of things I like about myself."

"Oh. How many do you have to have?"

"At least ten."

"How many do you have so far?"

"None." She handed me the last dish to dry, pulled the plug in the sink, dried her hands, and walked away.

None?

◆ ◆ ◆ ◆

I started my own assignment for Mrs. Killian before I went to bed. I made three columns on a sheet of paper and labeled them: *How to help Mom and Dad, How to help Carrie,* and *How to help myself.*

Don't cover for Carrie went in all three columns. The way I figured it, not having that responsibility had to help me, too.

Next, I used Mrs. Killian's suggestion. *Cooperate with counseling.* That went in all three columns, too.

Then under Mom and Dad's column, I wrote: *Remind them to spend time together.* They let things slip sometimes. I didn't think it would hurt to give them a little reminder once in a while.

For Carrie, I added: *Help her see the good things about herself.* She definitely needed help there.

I couldn't think of anything to add to my own column, just what Mrs. Killian said: *Be good to yourself, Amy.*

But how, Mrs. Killian? How?

Chapter
fourteen

I don't know what happened to the dress. It was hanging in my closet one day, and the next thing I knew, it was gone. I asked Mom about it, but she said, "Don't worry, Amy. Everything's been taken care of."

And when I mentioned it to Carrie, she said something really weird. She said that the dress was part of yesterday, and yesterday was gone. Then she added, "I've done a lot of things I'm not proud of, things I don't want to talk about."

I could understand that last part. I've done things I don't want to talk about either, but it didn't seem fair. I deserved to know where that dress came from, and what had happened to it. After all, I was the one who had worn it.

Maybe someday, I told myself. Maybe someday, when Carrie and I grow up and we have kids of our own and one of them is planning to go to the eighth-grade spring dance, maybe then she'll look at me and say, "Remember that dress you wore . . .?" And she'll tell me the whole story.

Maybe someday. But then something told me that that would never happen. Something told me that there was a part of Carrie I'd never know, a part of her I'd never understand.

◆ ◆ ◆ ◆

When my parents finally got around to asking about the play, Carrie answered for me. She told them what had happened and that it was her fault I didn't get the part. They told me that Carrie wasn't the only one to blame.

"We should have been more involved," Mom said. "We're sorry."

"We should have been paying closer attention," Dad said. "Then maybe it wouldn't have happened."

They weren't alone. I was sorry, too. Sorry I hadn't taken the audition more seriously. Sorry I didn't realize how important that play was to me. Sorry I'd let the whole thing slip through my fingers.

I shoved the thoughts out of my head and concentrated on other things. And after weeks of yelling and screaming and long hours of silence, it seemed my family was slowly turning around.

Mom and Dad stretched their walks to an hour. When they finally started hanging that wallpaper, I actually heard them laugh!

And when Carrie announced that she wanted to become a volunteer in the pediatric ward at the hospital, I almost fell over. "Don't act so shocked," she said. "Those kids need me. Who else is going to play checkers with them?"

And me—well, I spent a lot of time with David and Lisa. They were the best friends anyone could have and we always had fun together. But I knew there was an emptiness inside of me that they just couldn't fill.

I couldn't understand what that emptiness was all about until our local newspaper ran a story about the play. Rehearsals had started and there were pictures of the actors (including Vanessa) and an interview with Mr. Williams. He said that *West Side Story* was the biggest production the Community Theater had ever done, and that tickets were already selling "like hot cakes," and that the entire cast and crew were looking forward to opening night.

Opening night. You got butterflies in your stomach and your hands got sweaty and you felt like you were going to split in half. But when the curtain went up you forgot all about that. You were someone else, living another life, and when you were finished, you heard the applause. There wasn't another feeling in the world like it.

But it wasn't just the applause I was thinking about as I read the paper. There was something about being part of a play, something about watching it take shape before your eyes. There was something about that whole thing that made you feel like you belonged to it. And I knew it didn't matter if you had any lines to say. Just being there, just being part of it—that's all that counted.

Be good to yourself, Amy. Mrs. Killian's words mingled with the newsprint. I sat and thought for a long time. And then I did something I never thought I'd do.

I picked up the phone and called Mr. Williams.

"This is Amy Phillips," I told him. "I was just reading about the play in the newspaper. I know this is kind of late. I mean, I know rehearsals have started and everything. But I was thinking about what you said about being an extra? And, well, I was wondering if I could still—"

"Yes," he said, and I heard him smile.

I think I've got it now, Mrs. Killian.

I think I understand.

About the Author

JANET DAGON'S dream when she was young was to become a nurse. After she graduated from college, she worked as a nurse in a hospital. Then she left to become a full-time mother. It wasn't until after she had her youngest son that she began to write professionally. She has written articles for magazines, but fiction is her first love.

Janet gets most of her ideas for her books and short stories by asking the question, "What if?" When she was watching a TV report about runaways, she asked herself what it would be like to have your older sister run away from home. That question led to her first novel, *MISSING: Carrie Phillips, Age 15*. This book, *Don't Tell Mom,* continues the story of Carrie and Amy.

Janet lives in Pottsville, Pennsylvania, with her husband David and her three sons, Mark, Jeff, and Scott. When she's not writing, she enjoys reading, doing needlepoint, taking long walks, playing board games, and watching people.